THE GIFTED SISTERS AND THE GOLDEN MIRROR

RACHEL CRIST

Laura,

May you always
Embrace your SPARK!

— Rachel Crist

CONTENTS

COPYRIGHT

THE GIFTED SISTERS AND THE GOLDEN MIRROR

is a work of fiction.

Cover art and design by Chrissy at Damonza © 2018

Erets World Map by Rachel Crist © 2018

Acknowledgment for map brushes and images goes to Ron Frisby

First Edition

❀ Created with Vellum

DEDICATION

To my mother and father.
I love you more
And
Everyone dies.

1

LIVIA

I STAND near the top of an ancient pine, my long black hair spiraling high into the air. The cool winds have drifted down from Wolfmere Peak and I've spent the whole morning listening to pine needles rustle softly in the wind. I sigh along with them.

I'll turn sixteen in two days. Even though the day shouldn't feel different than any other, the itch to leave has gotten stronger. The Black Pines are the one place I've always been able to go to clear my head. They've been my home—but lately they've felt more like my prison.

The pines surround me, stretching out for miles. For centuries these trees have thrived, from as far back as when magic once covered our land, when mystical plants and creatures were found and all four kingdoms flourished on their gifts given by the Guardians of Maker Adon.

I cautiously brace myself on the sturdy limbs below me, knowing that a fall from this far up would mean my death. By now, Amah will be looking for me. I sink back down into the shelter of the pine and grab my pack to begin my descent.

I should've been back hours ago. But I got bored, scaled a

tree, and daydreamed my day away. I hadn't wanted to carry out mundane chores. I was in desperate need of an adventure.

"*Liiiivia!*"

My foot slips, causing me to slide down to the branch below. Scaly plates of bark flake away from the scrape of my boots. I squint through the limbs, and see Amah's thin frame stalking my way. I already can see the disappointment etched on her face.

When both of my parents died, Amah brought me to the Black Pines, taking it upon herself to raise me as her own. She's my caretaker, and her expectations of me have always been high. I've never understood why, and it's annoyingly suffocating. But this is the way it's always been.

Continuing down to the lowest branch, I brace my hands against the trunk and push off. Pine needles cushion my landing.

"You found me!" I announce.

Amah startles, and I grin. It's rare I ever catch her off guard.

Her brow angles down over the slant of her eyes, causing my grin to falter. More winds gust through, blowing her cropped hair into a black-spiked mess. With her serious expression, I find the combination rather amusing. I bite the inside of my cheek, trying not to laugh. I know better than to test her patience.

"It'll be dark soon. Let's go." Her words are crisp and harsh. Even though she often comes across this way, she's never outright punished me. Her disappointed looks are punishment enough. I follow after her.

Our cottage is tucked deep within the Black Pines between Wolfmere Peaks and Horn Lake, a plentiful area for us to hunt and fish. The closest village is a ride of two days to Kale, where we travel every other month to barter and trade. It's the only other place I've ever been.

We always stay at the same inn, talk with the same people, and go to the same stores. No matter how many times I carefully plan something different, Amah is right there, guiding me right back to her calculated schedule. It's a struggle to break free.

Amah says she's simply never found a reason to go anywhere else or do anything different. I've told her I want to travel to the capital city of Pynth, to see Willobourne Castle, where our kings and queens once dwelled. The stories I've heard paint a picture of a wondrous place that can only be magical—chock full of adventure I am dying to have.

But she always denies my requests; she refuses to go back to a home she barely escaped from. A home my parents knew, before they died in a raid brought by the erratic king in the East, almost sixteen years ago now. That unfortunate raid is what has kept me out here in seclusion my whole life.

To this day, Amah doesn't speak much about the night my parents died, but from what I've gathered through the years, it was my father who commanded her to leave during the raid, and to take me with her. When I asked why he'd asked her, she only said she was our family's protector, and left it at that.

I know she carries the guilt of leaving my parents behind, and it pains her to speak of them. But I love when she shares her rare stories of them. It is always on those nights when the weather doesn't allow us to go outside. We sit in front of the fire, and she tells me about the life of the castle.

My parents were the High Healers to the king and queen of the Western Kingdom. They gathered plants and herbs outside the city, where fields upon fields of plant life were grown and harvested. They knew how to make remedies that could keep our rulers healthy and treat them when sick. They carried on the much-imitated tradition of healing that our whole kingdom once possessed.

I used to think it was exciting how close my parents were to the king and queen. But the more I think about it, the more I wonder if my parents would still be alive if they hadn't worked for them. After all, the raiders came after the king and queen—not my parents.

I don't remember anything about my parents, but I've always hoped to become a High Healer like them one day. There isn't a king or queen anymore in our kingdom—for only a descendant of our true Guardians can sit on the throne. Regent Grif rules in their place, waiting for the missing heir. He's a Northern Prince, brother to the late queen.

A gust of wind sweeps my hair into my face, and before I have time to push it aside, I bump into Amah. I stumble back but she catches me by the arm. Her eyes narrow, looking off into the distance. I follow her gaze, but I don't see or hear anything.

Without a word, she continues on, and promptly picks up the pace until we are almost home. Soon enough, we are passing the shed where we keep our everyday supplies. It isn't anything fancy, but the thatched roof and pine walls give it plenty of character.

"I think I'll go fetch some wood for the fire."

If anything, gathering wood will show that I've accomplished something today—unlike the berries I forgot to pick.

She eyes me curiously, her lips set in a thin line.

"That would be wise, but don't linger too long."

I walk along the raked dirt, and head towards the shed. It's a walk I've made thousands of times. But I no longer want to repeat these steps. I can't live the rest of my life out here.

If only I could truly become a High Healer. And even if I didn't manage to become a High Healer, I could train to be something else—anything to be around other people.

It's not that I haven't enjoyed being raised by Amah. She has been good to me. But I long to see so much more.

All I know is from our past. Now I want to use the present to build a life in the future. But I can never tell this to Amah. She would never understand.

Once when I was reading one of the books on Amah's shelf, I found a passage that spoke of the mission of our Maker Adon. When he created our world of Erets, he sent four Guardians to establish his four kingdoms. He did it so we could live free—not be stuck in one place. Yes, each kingdom had its own specific gift, but he hoped we would all work together. Living separately we could not survive. And that has stuck with me ever since.

That was written when magic flowed throughout each kingdom, and the people all worked alongside one another. The kingdoms flourished until something horrible happened to change everything. And Maker Adon's dream fell to pieces.

I notice the shed door is ajar as I approach. The hairs on my arms rise. It's rare the door isn't securely fastened—there have only been those few times that squirrels have managed to break through.

I push the door farther in. Slipping inside, I peer around but see nothing out of place. I relax my posture, feeling foolish for thinking the worst. It's not as if anyone would actually be in here.

I go to the back of the shed where the firewood is stacked neatly against the wall, and begin stacking some in the crook of my arm. If this winter is anything like the last, I'm not looking forward to the long days trapped inside.

The shed moans against the wind, mirroring my thoughts. Who knows, maybe this winter I can weasel more stories out of Amah, and add them to my store of fond memories I could've had myself.

My arms are full, and I turn to leave. The light from outside shifts, sending shadows flickering across the floor. An imprint on the dirt floor catches my attention. Shifting the weight in my arms, I lean to get a closer look. A large footprint dusts the ground, and I realize quickly it's neither mine nor Amah's.

Out beyond the shed walls, a scream slices through my puzzlement.

The firewood falls from my arms, crashing to the ground. I dash out from the shed. Amah has never screamed before and fear fills me. What could have caused her to scream?

I run to the back side of our quaint cottage. My eyes dart around searching for Amah, and when they don't find her, I make my way around to the front.

I stop. Amah is pinned to the ground. A burly man in a hooded black cloak hovers over her. A sharp blade is in his hand, pointed at her breast. Amah's blade is out of reach on the ground next to her.

Amah's eyes burn with anger. When they shift to mine, the man turns his head to follow. On his face, there's a red mask. Fear tightens inside my chest. This is no ordinary intruder. This is a Silent Watcher!

I unsheathe my knife from my boot. My heart pounds inside my chest and I'm unsure of what to do next. There's no way I can take down a man this size. And with a knife? Amah has always made me carry this knife, but I have fallen short on how to wield it—unlike my bow. But the bow is too far away.

I shift the knife's handle between the tips of my fingers and throw it as hard as I can at the red-masked assassin. He brings his arm up to block it. Suddenly, Amah thrusts up and jams a concealed knife into the thick of his neck.

Without releasing a single cry, the light leaves the Silent Watcher's eyes. His body slumps forward, and Amah quickly moves out from beneath him.

I stare wide-eyed at the unmoving form splayed on the ground. Amah stands, and wipes blood from her knife. I watch as she tucks it away and then goes to collect her blade.

I study my hands. A sick feeling brushes over me. Amah motions for me to come help her. I stumble my way over to the dead body. How did this all happen? No one is supposed to know where we live.

The strong scent of iron hits my nose. Unable to restrain myself, my stomach lurches and I dash away, emptying my stomach's contents near a rose bush we planted last spring.

Amah's footsteps come closer.

"Go inside."

"I'm so sorry, Amah." Shame washes over me as I turn to face her.

"There is nothing to be sorry for, En Oli. Now go inside. Warm yourself by the fire, I'll be in shortly." She brushes her thumb across my cheek, then turns and walks away.

En Oli is a nickname she's used for as long as I can remember. It means My Light. Whenever I was scared or anxious, she would only have to call me by that name and my inner turmoil would calm. It comes from a lost language that is derived from that of her ancestors, who lived outside the four kingdoms in the Tar Islands.

I know she used it to calm me, but it isn't working. Not now. I fear the Silent Watchers. I walk up the wooden steps to our home, and go inside.

I sit down on my favorite wooden chair, one lined with fur, and tuck my feet up underneath me. We haven't heard a whisper from these assassins for years. That one of them has found his way to our makeshift life is beyond unsettling. Silent Watchers were the ones who raided my family's home, and murdered them. These men are the reason Amah has kept us hidden away.

I thought we were safe.

I thought wrong.

As flames dance in the hearth, I think back to the lessons

I've had on the Watchers. How those lessons frightened me. But Amah was insistent that I know about the evil ways of the Eastern Kingdom, the place where the Silent Watchers are trained to kill.

The Silent Watchers serve King Kgar. They are the merciless shadows that do his bidding. They constantly try to penetrate our kingdom, hoping to find our weakness.

It's why The Wall was built. The Western and Northern Kingdoms fought against the Eastern Kingdom, forcing The Wall up to keep the invaders in the mountains to the east. A single gate was built to allow limited bartering and trading of goods. But that's it.

It's why it came as a shock when they succeeded in their raid against us sixteen years ago. Come to find out, the Southern Kingdom's Enchanter had been aiding them.

A bright light outside snaps me out of my thoughts. I go look out the window, and see a large fire tickling the night sky. Amah stands nearby, watching the flames.

I squint towards the fire to see what she's burning. An unsettling feeling comes, and I'm afraid I know the answer. The flames part just enough, and I see the assassin's body.

I hurry back to my chair, terrified. Minutes later, the front door opens. Amah trudges inside, shutting the door firmly behind her. I watch her as she pulls off her outer layers, her cheeks already pink from the cold. She steps over to the fire and begins to warm her hands.

I don't know why I'm so unsettled by her actions. I should've been able to put it all together. A master in weaponry, a protector to my family. I just can't imagine her harming anyone, let alone killing someone. It is something that goes firmly against my very being. I can't exactly explain it. It is something that just runs through my veins.

A shudder skitters down my spine, and I shove it away. I can't focus on the actual killing. It was a tense situation, and there was no way around it. I know this.

Amah turns slowly; the light behind her casts her face into shadow.

"It's no longer safe here. We'll leave tomorrow."

Words I've so longed to hear are finally spoken. But I fear it won't be the adventure I've envisioned.

2

VERA

SILENCE HOVERS over the colossal arena. Silent Watchers stand behind me, observing me as I stare at the wooden target up ahead. I release the knife in my hand. It whips through the air, hitting its mark twenty paces away. Picking up another knife, I throw again. *Thunk.* It sticks hard, landing a hairsbreadth from the first. I wipe my brow on my sleeve. It's barely dawn, and already I'm sweating. The subtle breeze barely gives me relief.

Murrow hands me five more knives and nods firmly. After having spent most of our training together, he knows I've got this.

I take a deep breath. A single mistake will cost me. One after another, I flick each knife. They twirl beautifully, hitting the target dead center. The corner of my mouth tugs upward —perfect.

Cheers and groans erupt behind me. Murrow pats me on the back.

"Brilliant, Vera." He grins, showing the small gap between his two front teeth. He runs to collect the knives, his narrow strip of brown hair catching the breeze.

Behind me, a small group of new Silent Watchers grumble

as they hand over their losing bets to my other friends, Karl and Nate. They are both muscular, and I try not to laugh when I see them flexing their arms, trying to intimidate the recruits into giving them more money.

The four of us all started in the same recruiting class many years ago. We were only eight at the time, we knew we would be friends the moment we all chose similar knives to practice with—but our friendship was risky.

King Kgar has never approved of my happiness. I've tried to run my friends off many times, trying to keep them out of harm's way, but they've never budged. Now, years later, I'm glad they never gave up on me. Even if they did use me at times.

Nate decided to use my skills this morning to earn a quick coin. He knew this new group of assassins wouldn't know any better. How were they to know a girl could throw better than any assassin in Graves Hill? It was easy money. He and Karl enjoy sneaking into town to gamble.

A Silent Watcher's life is one of vigilant training. The king's rules are strongly enforced and my friends are lucky not to have been caught. Unlike for them, the king's eyes are constantly on me, one way or another. I've had no choice but to be smart. There are only a few things I've ever managed to get away with, and sneaking into the city of Dryden to gamble is not worth it to me.

The sour-faced Watchers groan as they depart. Nate flicks a coin towards me, and I snatch it out of the air hoping for silver. My face falls when my open hand reveals a copper.

"You know, if you guys plan on dragging me out of bed early, it better be worth more than this."

"It's not about the money," Murrow says. "It's about the glory," He comes back over carrying my knives. Rolling my eyes, I take my knives and tuck them in my belt—along with the worthless coin.

Looking up, I squint to see Nate's face towering high

above me. Grinning widely, he reminds me of an oversized child. His blond hair curls up at the nape of his neck, and his cheeks have dimples on both sides. I hear the girls in Dryden find him quite handsome. And even though I can see it, I can never look at him that way. He's family.

"I hope you're not asking for a raise, Vera."

I roll my eyes again, and Nate barks out a laugh. His eyes shift past me, and he stills.

Turning around, I see where Nate is staring. The morning light reflects off the Commander's shiny bald head. His stern gaze hides under the bushiest of eyebrows I've ever seen. He's the king's uncle, and the leader of the king's forces.

Commander Bellek's long strides lead directly to me. Nate knows better than to move an inch; in fact, we all know better. Catching the attention of the Commander is never a good thing. Loose hairs escape my braid and tickle across my face. But I remain still.

"Commander Bellek, Sir!" We shout in unison. A drum starts up from the middle of the arena. He looks us up and down with a practiced suspicion, then holds out his hand.

"Hand it over."

Nate steps around me, placing the sack of coins in the Commander's hand and falls back beside me. The beat of the drum continues on.

"Well, what are you waiting for? Don't you hear the drums? Stations!"

Clasping our wrists to our chests, we respond together, "Yes, Commander!"

"Except you, Vera."

Inwardly grimacing, I remain in place as the others dash away. I lift my head, and jut out my chin.

"How much did you get from the new recruits?" he asks.

"I didn't get a chance to ask. We were interrupted."

His expression remains placid, clearly unimpressed by my smart retort.

"You're lucky I like your ugly face. That mouth of yours is nothing but trouble."

Puffing out my chest, I grin.

When King Kgar captured me, he had no desire to raise me himself so he handed me over to his uncle, Bellek. Not having a clue how to raise a girl, he raised me the only way he knew how: I became a trained assassin. In return, I trained him. I taught him that raising a girl isn't easy.

"It's funny how Nate towers over you, yet you still manage to make him shake in his boots," I observe.

"At least the boy knows his place. Maybe you could learn from him."

I scowl.

Silent Watchers start pouring into the enormous arena that's been built into mountain sides, alert to the sound of the drums. The drum's cadence signals the start of training. Everyone has until the last beat to arrive at their stations. There are exactly one hundred beats. If they are late, they are sent immediately to the whipping block—which isn't a good way to start your day.

"Now get to your station. I can't have you whipped before your birthday."

My birthday's tomorrow. King Kgar plans a lavish celebration of it every year. Sparing no expense. I'm never thrilled about this day, for I've no desire to be paraded in front of a room full of noblemen and their pompous wives. But I have no choice.

To the people, I am the property of the king and to be treated as such. No one's allowed to talk directly to me, or touch me. In the arena, however, the rules do not apply. It's the one place I can escape the invisible chains of the king.

I weave through the thousands of Silent Watchers—a black sea of strength and power. Everyone wears their black threads, an impenetrable fabric that's made in the Tar Islands.

There are four main stations spaced out around the arena.

Archery, sword skills, knife throwing, and the cages. The cages are where I head to now.

Some would say it is strange that I train with the men who helped murder my real family, but having never known my parents, it is hard to feel hate. I've been raised by these men, and strangely enough they're my family now.

I know all the details of my capture and the murder of my parents. But it's the king who ordered the raid, and it will always be the king that I hate. Plus, only one assassin survived that raid, so I can't hold these assassins accountable for something they didn't do.

My lungs burn as I hurry across the arena. Dirt kicks out from under my boots. Graves Hill is the largest training arena in all the four kingdoms. It is built into Wolfmere Peaks, the treacherous mountain range that towers up high over the arena, its tips hidden in the clouds.

Thousands of men train here daily, and every day is different. As the only female, I've had to prove my worth to these men. With my knife throwing skills, I've earned my place. They don't view me as the "prisoner" the way the king and the rest of kingdom do. In their eyes, I fight just as hard and receive the same proud scars they do, so they view me the same—family.

The drum stops and I slow my pace, stopping at the edge of my station. I rest my hands on my knees, breathing heavily. Just in time.

I maneuver through the men as everyone circles around thick iron bars. Being shorter than most, I'm determined to get a good view. Sparring is the best kind of entertainment. Even with the strict rules.

There are three rules for the cage. No weapons, spectator silence, and no interference. Violate any of these three, and you are sent straight to the whipping block.

Captain Ryker stands alone inside. His red hair slicks back perfectly, not a single hair out of place. Straight-edged sideburns come down alongside his rugged jaw, and he is displaying his normal unimpressed expression.

He waits for us to gather around before he chooses the first two assassins who are to fight. Ryker is unforgiving. He, of course, has his favorites, and I'm not one of them.

My eyes dart around, sizing everyone up. No one is even close to my size, not even the new recruits. This has always been a problem for me, and it's why the cage is my least polished skill. Reaching back, I pull my braid forward over my shoulder and adjust the red band around my head. No matter how hard I fight, it's never enough against the weight of these muscled men.

Captain Ryker points out two assassins to begin the day. They make their way towards the gate, dropping their weapons at the entrance. Barely giving them time to reach the center, Ryker signals the fight.

Both men crouch down. The bigger of the two makes the first lunge. His opponent moves quickly, sidestepping his advance. The bigger one lunges again, and throws himself at the other's legs. Not able to escape this time, his opponent is slammed to the ground. The fighter on top brings his fist down hard. *Crack.* Blood pours from the opponent's nose. He tries to scramble out, but to no avail.

I peer around, curious to see whom I might face. So many intently watch the fight inside the cage—except for one. Beyond the fighters, and on the other side of the cage, there are two piercing blue eyes staring directly into mine— Marcus. He winks and my skin flushes. A memory of tangled sheets and warm lips against my neck floods my mind. His perfect mouth curves up into a playful grin. He is my forbidden secret.

I turn my focus back to the fight. I can't have him distracting me, even if I'd rather be sparring with him someplace else.

Bloody nose hasn't managed to get back up, and has just been issued a hard kick to his side. I shake my head.

Ryker steps forward and calls the fight. He looks at the weak assassin as if he were a disease. "Whipping block," he spits. The losing assassin drags himself up and limps out of the cage towards the center of the arena. I don't envy him one bit; I've taken that humiliating walk more times than I can count.

A shadow passes overhead and I peer up. A large cloud creeps its way across the sky, blocking out the unrelenting sun. My eyes close and I embrace the rare shade. Please, let more clouds come. Unfortunately, the East is somehow cursed with the sun's merciless kiss.

Ryker's smirk greets me when my eyes open—shit. He points to me, choosing me for the next fight. Not caring who I'm up against, I go to the gate and drop my weapons. I brush my braid back over my shoulder as I enter the cage.

I ignore Ryker, and stride past him. I crack my neck and shake out my hands before facing my opponent. Standing before me is Kah. I glare at the captain—really, Ryker?

Kah is Ryker's main crony. He's a giant, with massive arms the size of tree trunks. Whenever Ryker needs things taken care of, he sends Kah. So many times he's whispered threats under his breath, and those are the only times I am thankful for King Kgar's strict rules about touching me—even if they don't stop the leering glances that come my way. Because even the assassins have limits in place when it comes to me.

Ryker signals us to start. Not wasting any time, Kah runs straight for me and I dive quickly to the side. Sand scatters around me as I quickly jump back up. Instead of chasing after me, Kah stands beyond me and smirks. I know he's playing with me and my annoyance flares. The sun peeks through the grey clouds, casting light over Kah's pock-marked face. Big *and* ugly.

Not letting him get to me, I sprint back towards him. He squats down, preparing for my advance. I slide in front of him at the last second, kicking sand in his face. He flinches back and I slide through his legs while he rubs the sand away from his eyes. I jump up quickly and slam my foot hard against his right leg. He grunts as he goes to his knees and I wrap my arm around his neck.

Squeezing with all my strength, I know it won't be enough. Kah reaches up and grabs my arm. He pulls down hard, overpowers me, and flips me up over his shoulder. I slam hard against the ground. Air is knocked from my lungs and before I can breathe, he yanks me close, throws his leg over, and straddles me.

Trying to catch my breath, I try to wiggle away. He pins my arms above me and lowers his face to mine. His breath reeks and I turn my head to the side. Anger rolls over me as his lips brush my ear.

"I always wanted to view you the way King Kgar does."

My eyes flash. Turning back to him, I spit in his face. Kah grips my hair and pulls my head back. A cry escapes my lips. Kicking out my legs, I try to twist away from him. But Kah is solid. I'm going nowhere.

Ryker steps forward. "Enough."

Kah's upper lip curls and he whispers words only I can hear. "You are lucky that your pretty little face is protected by the king." He pushes my head into the ground and rolls off me.

Breathing heavily, I scramble away. I push my hair off my face, and spit sand out from my mouth. "Lucky me."

Captain Ryker sneers. I see nothing short of disgust on his face.

"Get out of my sight." He crosses his arms. "And don't forget to visit the whipping block."

I bite my tongue. It isn't worth giving him fuel. It will all come back and burn me later. So I exit the cage, retrieving my weapons before storming off.

Hoofbeats sound in the distance. Shielding my eyes from the sun, I strain to see who approaches. Two brown horses gallop towards me and the blood drains from my face when I see the lone rider.

It's the most vicious Silent Watcher of them all—Bruce of Tar. Not only is he the king's personal bodyguard, but he's also the one surviving assassin who killed my parents.

Pulling up short, Bruce stares through the two slits in his red mask—a mask I've never seen him without. A grotesque scar peeks out from underneath it and runs down his chin to his collar bone. I've always hoped it's a scar made by my father.

Knowing he is here for me, I close the distance and mount up on the spare horse. Without a word, Bruce tugs his horse around and takes off. I might be saved from the whipping block for now, but my destination won't be any better.

Glancing back over my shoulder, Bellek stands on the dais near the drum. His black cape flutters loosely around him, and his grim expression causes my throat to tighten.

Squeezing my heels against the horse's side, I ride after Bruce. No matter how fast I go, I'll inevitably be late. Unaware of what this summons could mean, fear twists in my gut, as I am taken to the king.

3

LIVIA

"WHAT DO YOU MEAN, tomorrow? Are you afraid more will come?" I ask.

Leaning forward, Amah reaches down and unlaces her boots, wincing from the stiffness in her hands. For years now, she has spent her evenings massaging them, trying to work out each laborious day's ache.

"We leave tomorrow because I fear for you."

"I don't understand."

A shadow passes over her face.

"There was once a prophecy. I've never told you of it, because I don't believe in prophecy. It speaks of a descendant who will bring magic back to our world. A descendant of Queen Bellflower."

"*The* Queen Bellflower? The most powerful queen in all the four kingdoms, the one born with all four gifts? *That* queen?"

"Yes, that one."

"How does a Silent Watcher coming out to the middle of the Black Pines have anything to do with Queen Bellflower? She's been dead for a hundred years."

"It's time I told you of the night Willobourne Castle was raided."

I know she means the night my parents died. For so long I've wanted to know. But dread decides to take shape inside me, and I fear how her story will unfold.

"I'll start by telling you how much King Helm and Queen Kyra were loved deeply by the people. And no one loved the people more than they. The people begged them for years to produce an heir, and the king and queen wanted to, but the queen found herself barren. It was heart-wrenching for both the queen and her people. However, King Helm wouldn't leave his beloved queen subjected to the depression that befell her. He called on the most unexpected person you could imagine—the Enchanter."

"What! Why would he do such a thing?"

"Quiet. Let me finish. The Enchanter agreed and sent forth a Woman of the Scree."

I grit my teeth. The Women of the Scree are creatures created by the Enchanter himself. They aren't even human, but magical puppets that the Enchanter can control from afar. Our kingdom has been forbidden to have any dealings with them.

"When the Woman of the Scree first arrived, no one knew. She went in and out with no one knowing any the better. But I knew. I was there. This moment is what put the prophecy in play in the mind of the Eastern King. He discovered the Western Queen had become pregnant, and was told the child would be the heir to bring back magic.

To our king's dismay, he uncovered the alliance between King Kgar and the Enchanter too late. I was in the nursery that night when the two assassins came in. I fought with all my strength and I almost died. But the king saved me. He had already been fatally wounded, and he still managed to keep me safe—and you.

"Me? Why would he save me?"

"Before I answer your question, you must understand I had reasons not to share this with you."

"Okay…"

She closes her eyes, and takes in a pained breath. "They wanted you, because they wanted the heir."

"Did I share a room with the heir?"

"No. Your father commanded me to escape with you, because your father was King Helm, and you were his daughter."

My mouth opens but nothing comes out—my thoughts are frozen. A silence fills the room.

"It's impossible, what you are saying."

"It's not, En Oli. It's the truth."

"So I'm the heir? *The* heir?"

Amah nods.

A rush of emotions passes through me.

"How am I supposed to believe this? King Helm and Queen Kyra were my parents? *My* parents? This whole time you've lied to me? Now I have to believe my parents were actually the king and queen? What's next—that there isn't truly a High Healer position to begin with?"

Her silence answers me, causing a tightness to form inside my chest. I no longer know what to think. Our reasons for living here are shrouded in lies. Amah isn't hiding here for her own fear of the Silent Watchers. She hides so the Eastern King won't find me. And with my parents dead, it makes the Western Kingdom—mine. I'm the missing heir! A wave of nausea passes over me as I sit on the edge of my chair, resting my head in my hands.

"The Silent Watcher was here for me, wasn't he?"

"Yes."

"And you are afraid more will come?"

"Yes, more will come. It's why we must leave and go to Pynth. Go back to where you can get Regent Grif's protection."

My throat closes up, unsure of how to feel. I feel a sort of denial of it all, like a dream that I will soon wake up from. I look out the window. The sun is long gone, and the darkness will soon turn to morning—reminding me again, we will soon be leaving.

"Why did you keep this from me? Did you ever plan on telling me?"

"I was planning on telling you one day—all of it. Each time I tried, words failed me. You're too smart for your own good, and I knew you would put it all together. And I knew you'd be hunted. I wasn't ready to place that fear inside you. But I wanted you to know the Eastern ways so that when I did tell you, you'd understand the seriousness of what I am doing for you. Never doubt the love of your parents, or the sacrifice they made for you. The only thing that changes are the crowns they wore. I'm sorry I kept this from you." Amah clears her throat. "I also wanted to wait to see if the prophecy spoke truth."

"I thought you didn't believe in prophecy."

"I don't, but I've always believed in magic's return."

"Well, as of right now, I don't have any magic. If I am supposed to have it, when should it appear?"

"I don't know."

"Will it be the lost healing gift of our kingdom?"

"Another question I don't know the answer to. I'm sorry."

I remember as a little girl pretending to be Queen Bell-flower. She is the only queen in all the four kingdoms to have had all four gifts.

I would pretend rocks were small creatures that were injured, and that I could use our Western Kingdom's gift to heal them.

With the Northern gift, I would pretend to freeze trees in place, mimicking the gift's physical manipulation. But when it came to using the Southern gift, I would make Amah frustrated, for I would cover myself in mud to become invisible and hide for the whole day—that is until my stomach grumbled and gave me away.

I never liked to play pretend with the Eastern gift of undeniable strength. The Easterners killed our people and I refused to be a murderer. But to really have even one of these gifts? How does one even fathom that?

"Sleep on this, En Oli. Tomorrow we'll have plenty of time to talk. I'm sorry for the secrets, but I'm glad you now know."

We stand, I wrap my arms around her, and rest my head against her chest.

"I don't know how to feel right now. But I understand. Thank you for keeping me safe."

She squeezes me tight and for a moment I sense she is going to say something else. But she doesn't. I go to my room and slip under my covers. Tomorrow we leave. And we will most likely never return.

THE NEXT MORNING, I drum my fingers along the windowsill and watch tiny flakes of snow trickle down from the sky. It must've been falling all night for it to have covered everything in sight. I search for any traces of yesterday, but find nothing.

Adjusting my quiver and bow on my shoulder, I head outside. Amah was awake when I got up, and of course everything is ready to go. All she has left to do is to bring Rosie out from the barn and hitch her to the wagon. While she does this, I decide to get one last round of arrows in before we leave.

I pull my cloak tight around me, and cold wind licks my face as I step off the porch and head towards the barn. Like the shed, it also has plenty of character. Built of aged pine, it has taken repetitive beatings from my arrows. Rosie might not have enjoyed the continuous thump against her home, but over time she's embraced it as an everyday part of her life.

I stop fifty paces out from the backside of the barn, the one place designated for me. Sliding an arrow out of my quiver, I set it and pull back the string. As I have so many times before, I release it without having to think. I've been shooting since I was seven. It is just another extension of myself.

The arrow slices through the brittle air, hitting the worn-down target, sending chips of paint flaking away. I grab another arrow.

Waking up this morning was surreal and somewhat painful. Sleeping on the revelations from last night, however, was the best thing I could've done. Knowing that we would soon be heading to safety, I was able to embrace my excitement for everything else.

Surprisingly, knowing the truth of my parents wasn't all that bad. This is something I know I will eventually be able to accept. The reason why they died, however, is the hardest part to swallow. It brings all of known history to bear on my own reality, and it's caused a hole to form inside my heart. I can only hope that I will manifest the gift of healing, because that will be the only thing to mend it.

I continue sending arrows one after another. Soon they are all bunched together in the center.

"I will rely on that aim if we run into any trouble."

I turn around. Amah is standing there holding Rosie by her reins. I wonder how long she's been watching me.

"As long as it's my bow. That knife throw was horrible."

"Never doubt yourself, En Oli. You see it as a flaw, but I saw it as opportunity, and it saved my life. Now go gather your arrows. It's time to go."

I do as she says, then follow her back to the covered wagon, and watch her hitch Rosie in the harness.

I kick the snow from my boots and climb up onto the wagon and settle on the padded bench. Amah climbs up after me and without a single look back, she clicks her tongue and we move out.

I look back to the place I've called home my whole life. A heaviness sinks through me. A part of me will miss the memories made here. There is another part, though, that has longed for this adventure. Then again, here I could have been anything I wanted. No one here to judge. Soon I will be in a city where there will be expectations of me. A part of my soul imprints itself among the trees, knowing the Black Pines will always be a part of me, no matter where I am.

Amah rests her hand on my leg. Her face reflects my thoughts. She too will miss this place.

We travel the next few hours without much talk. My thoughts move between reminiscing on my past and chewing on my new-found future. At first I feel guilty for wanting to be excited about it all. I should be upset at Amah for hiding these truths from me. But being angry isn't something I am accustomed to and it won't get me anywhere, so I try to embrace my excitement instead.

"Does Regent Grif know I'm alive?"

"He does."

"Have you been in contact with him?"

"I have."

"Really?"

Amah sighs. "You know the Regent is a Northern Prince, right?"

"Yes."

"Where is your mother from?"

It's a question that gives me pause. My whole life I've thought of my mom as being from the West. But Queen Kyra is now my mother. And Queen Kyra was from the North.

"Are you saying Regent Grif is my uncle?"

"He is. And we've been exchanging messages your whole life."

"You've been in contact with him this whole time?" The

depth of this hidden truth strikes me. It is one thing, him knowing of me, but actively keeping up with me for sixteen years without my knowing? That's hurtful.

"Why didn't he reach out to me? If you were in contact with him this whole time, what kept him from bringing me back to Pynth?"

"I did."

"You did?"

"The city of Pynth needed to rebuild. I wasn't confident of the safety at Willobourne Castle. Regent has dedicated the last sixteen years to making Pynth strong again. He's been wanting you to return."

"So Regent Grif allowed you to tell him no?"

I would think that Amah would have no say in such matters. The Regent was just as powerful as a king. "What could've kept him from marching up to us and taking me away?"

"I used an evlock."

"A what?"

"An untraceable bird. I acquired one in a trade, in Kale. Annie keeps it for me."

Of course Annie does. Annie is Amah's sidekick of sorts. She owns the only inn in Kale, Bear Horn Inn. It wouldn't surprise me if she knew all about me.

There are many layers to Amah and I have a feeling there are more I will uncover before we reach Pynth. The open world will be a challenge for her, when all my life she has tried to keep me hidden away. In the morning I will be sixteen, and I am already on the adventure of my life.

4

VERA

FOR AS LONG AS I can remember, the mountainous terrain that we live in has forever trapped heat. Even now the ground smolders and sends up a disorientating haze as we head down the hill to Black Ridge Castle. And year round, occasional thunderstorms have kept us from completely drying out.

There are some who talk about how they wish our winters could be like those of the West. They say the snow can get as deep as you are tall there. I've never seen snow up close; sometimes I've seen white on the tops of mountains, but that's my only experience with the stuff.

As we get closer to the castle, the massive fortress seems dark and uninviting. It's made from the black obsidian stone mined in the peaks. It's a rare stone that holds special value to our kingdom; it's worth more than the diamonds and rubies that are also mined. However, the combination of the three allows the king to never have to worry about falling into poverty. Of course, one can't say how the rest of the kingdom is faring. Let's just say the king doesn't know how to share.

Servants take our horses the moment we arrive. Without waiting for Bruce, I head inside.

The castle is bustling with servants in every corridor. They're preparing for the oncoming celebration. Without a single glance my way, they move around me, focusing intently on the tasks at hand. They know what's in store for them if everything isn't perfect.

It's another year for the Eastern King to celebrate, hoping for it to finally be the year my magic manifests. I curse the Enchanter who issued the damn prophecy. Even more, that he sent a Woman of the Scree to live here. The king says she was a gift, but I know she's here to keep an eye on me. The Enchanter will want to know if someone other than he himself has any magic.

I only hope that whatever gift I receive, it will be something that allows me to escape this life of torment. Even if it means leaving my friends behind.

I enter the Throne Room—an enormous room with large black pillars. A single chandelier hangs down from the ceiling, an object I've wished many times to drop down upon the king. One of the many different fantasies I've cooked up over the years.

Historical tapestries hang along the walls, depicting the gruesome beheadings and whippings the people of this land have had to endure. The king never fails to remind people what could befall them. I hate it all.

King Kgar sits regally on a brilliant piece of forged art, built also from black obsidian stone. His throne is made from one solid piece, and the back arches up at least ten feet.

Placed on a raised dais, the height gives him the excuse to look down his long narrow nose and judge with his hooded, dark eyes.

As always, the Woman of the Scree sits next to him. Her cool, relaxed posture doesn't fool me. Her rich brown hair falls in layered waves past her shoulders, and down her voluptuous frame. She is a creature that captures the lust of any who gaze upon her. She's pure evil.

I bristle when her black voided eyes follow my every move. I can never tell when the Enchanter is watching through them. It was one of the many benefits the Enchanter gained when he sent the Scree out. He created them for this very reason—to spy. Therefore, I don't trust her.

The sneer on the king's face becomes more prominent the closer I get. The thump of my heart beats loud, and I try to find my center. His black robes drape around him flawlessly, his blond hair standing out in stark contrast to them.

Some say the king's sharp features are attractive, but I never could see it. His black soul is all I see, making him far from anything to admire.

A golden crown encrusted with large red rubies sits on his brow. His fingers are covered in ornate rings. He looks ridiculous.

A flash of curly blond hair jets out from behind a pillar, making a beeline straight for me. My heart melts as Zyrik runs and jumps into my arms. He is King Kgar's five year old son. His golden curls bounce around his angelic face. When he nuzzles my neck, the smell of the lavender he bathes in wafts in my face. The scent calms me. I set him down, and he immediately takes my hand.

Ignoring his son, Kgar stands and throws his arms out. "There she is, our very own Western Princess."

His voice is smooth but laced with ridicule. I hate how he mocks me. The constant reminder of who I am but will never become. The kidnapped princess who rules no one.

I've tried many times to run away, not caring when or how I'd be punished when caught. That is until Zyrik was born, and the king started using him as a form of my punishment.

"Your Majesty." I bow, keeping my eyes downcast. His gaze has always been disquieting, and even now his low chuckle signals his sense of my discomfort.

Stepping down off the dais, Kgar embraces me. He grazes his

hands slowly down my back, feeling me out. I keep the bile in the back of my throat. Before pulling away, his lips brush by my ear, and he whispers softly, "Make sure you behave, *my* princess."

He may have whispered, but the threat rings loud and clear. Sitting back on his throne, Kgar claps twice. The main doors open and in walk the noblemen on his council. Zyrik squeezes my hand, and I rub my thumb over his for comfort.

The nobles' rich robes fold around them as they bow to the king. Ignoring both me and Zyrik, they seat themselves on benches provided.

The king's council consists of twenty men. They are young noblemen, none older than the king. He wants no one on his council that knew his father, and he has hand-picked each one of them.

They are as ruthless as the king, taxing above what they should and taking the extra for themselves. They constantly suck up to the king, showering him with praises he doesn't deserve—but they also fear him. They'll never admit it though. Like me, they never know the king's mind or his intent, given his outlandish decisions.

As the last of the noblemen find their seats, the king stands once again. "As you all are aware, tomorrow marks a glorious day. We celebrate Princess Vera's birthday. Hopefully, this year will bring us back the gift of old that we have been patiently waiting for."

I grind my teeth. He's never been patient about this. After every celebration for the past fifteen years, I've been taken to his torture room, where he's shown me his disgust for my failure to manifest the gift.

"The Scree here has brought to my attention that once this gift manifests, our kingdom could be in grave danger from Vera's power."

The noblemen cast their judgment my way. I ignore them. "She has agreed to conjure up a binding agreement for Vera to sign. Of course, as she has brought this to my attention, I thought I would extend this binding agreement to my council to ensure my utmost safety."

The doors to the throne room open, and in marches a troop of Silent Watchers. They come and stand behind the noblemen. A sudden intensity thickens in the air around us. Zyrik drops my hand, and runs from the room.

"In this contract it is stated that if I am killed, then you will all die—as punishment for failing to protect me. The Enchanter himself has placed the locking spell on this contract, and it is unbreakable."

The room erupts into angry protests. Kgar flicks his wrist. A Watcher grabs a nobleman and forces him down to his knees. The flash of steel that grazes quickly across his throat prompts complete silence. I'm thankful Zyrik ran off when he did.

The king's eyes flash with excitement. "As for you, Vera, if you cause me any harm, your life will become forfeit to the Temple of the Scree and Zyrik will die."

His lips curl into a smile, challenging me to protest. Anger boils up inside me and I do my best to suppress my outrage. I can't take his bait. He knows Zyrik is my weakness, that I would do anything to keep him safe.

The thought of being banished to the Temple would seem to be better than living here, but it's not. The Southern Kingdom is never traveled. It's a desolate place in the desert lands, where the Temple of the Scree is hidden. The thought of living there sounds wretched. I can only imagine what the Enchanter would do with me.

Everyone knows the Enchanter was the one responsible for all the kingdoms losing their gifts. He has been around thousands of years, dabbling in the forbidden magical books left by Guardian Acadia.

Every part of me hates the idea of signing the king's

binding contract. It shows me how calculating he is—but the king knows he has me.

King Kgar points to an unfurled scroll lying on a table between him and the Scree. He cocks his head to the side, "Sign it."

Picturing one of my many knives going through his chest, I march over to the table, and sign. A warming sensation passes over me. The binding is complete.

NOT CARING whether he would dismiss me or not, I leave. Traveling quickly through the castle, I pass through the kitchens and descend the winding staircase to the forgotten chambers. This is where Zyrik will be.

Leakage and mold growth keeps most away from this part of the castle. Whoever built this side, didn't give much care to it, and over time it has decayed greatly. The musty smell tickles my nose and my ears perk up when I hear his small whimper coming from inside a large abandoned cabinet.

When King Kgar noticed how small Zyrik was when he was born, he wanted him dead. Drowned like a rat. His mother was a town whore, and only used to breed for the king. She was killed after giving birth. So I fought for him that day and I thought for sure the king would deny me. But the king knew a gambling opportunity when he saw one, and to this day he has used his son to influence my decisions.

I creep up close to the cabinet and knock gently three times. The whimpers stop and the door slowly opens.

Zyrik's bright blue eyes peek out. When he sees it's me, he jumps out, and embraces me fiercely.

"I knew I would find you, Little Rik." He pulls back to gaze into my face. "You sure are sneaky, hiding over here." He giggles quietly and lays his head against my chest.

Two years ago, I was summoned by the king for something I had done. When I arrived, he had Zyrik sitting on his lap. I remember Zyrik's precious smile. But he didn't know what his father had in store. Two Silent Watchers held me down as the king ran a sharp blade along the inside of Zyrik's arm. No matter how much Zyrik cried or tried to escape, the king held firm. I had to stand there and watch blood drip down his arm, past his chubby little fingers, and down to the floor. He screamed my name while tears streamed down his face. I couldn't save him. He hasn't spoken a single word since that day. His last word I recall vividly; he was screaming my name.

"I am sorry you had to be there to see your father be mean."

Zyrik sneaks a glance up to my face. He rolls back his sleeve and points to his scar, and then points to me.

"No, I don't plan on letting your father hurt me. It might seem that way, but I will not allow it."

Zyrik grins.

I know he doesn't fully understand all that's transpired, but that's fine with me. I would rather he not know.

"Let's get you back to your room. Is that okay, Little Rik?"

He smiles and nods.

By the time we get to his room, he's asleep in my arms. I tuck him into his bed and kiss his forehead.

"Love you always."

He doesn't move. I admire his long black eyelashes and his dimpled chin. I really hate how this little boy is my number one weakness. Seeing him suffer at my expense is a horrible way to watch him grow up.

So many times I've wished to run away with him. But fear grips me each time. Should we be caught, who knows how far the king would push his punishment. I shudder.

I kiss him gently on the head, and leave him to his peaceful dreams.

Looking out the windows on the way to my chambers, the sun is high in the sky. Down below, travelers and merchants move back and forth through Falcons Pass. The Pass was carved between two massive mountains. On the other side is the capitol city of Dryden, named after the Guardian of our kingdom. Though it is so close, I've never been there. Nate and Karl tell me I'm not missing much. "Only thieves and cheats litter that pisshole city," they say.

Upon entering my room, my fireplace is kindled. And it shouldn't be. I crouch low and unsheathe a blade. I survey the room and I hear a sound coming from my washroom. Slowly, I sneak across the room.

The door opens and out steps a tall muscular figure. I sweep my leg out, knocking him to the ground. Quickly, I straddle the intruder and place my blade at his throat.

"Holy hell, Vera! It's just me."

"Marcus?"

Sheathing my blade, I remain straddling him. He scowls.

"Oh, don't you get grumpy. It's not my fault you let me sneak up on you."

Marcus rolls his eyes. He bucks me forward and wraps his muscular arms around me. My face stops inches in front of his and I'm now fully aware of his bare chest and wet brown hair.

I attempt to sit up, but he locks his hold on me. His lips form a half smirk. I lick his nose and he quickly releases me.

"Aw, gross."

I push myself off him, and stand. As he wipes his face, I walk past him and close myself inside the washroom. I hear him mutter something, but I don't quite make out what it is. Something about me not being ladylike.

I unlace my corset and peel off my threads. My nose tingles at the smell of my own sweat. Reaching back to my braid, I loosen it free, and remove the red band from around my head; I was denied a red mask so I wear the band for my own personal status among the assassins.

After I wash the grime away, I stand in front of the full-length mirror. My eyes gaze over my scarred body. A bitterness fills my mouth. I don't remember a time when my body had none of these marks.

Of course, scars in our kingdom are worn proudly. They show others what you have survived. But for me, I despise most of them. Only because most of mine have came from the king.

It took a long time for me to let Marcus finally see me. He started to romance me over a year ago. I reminded him many times of the danger that even touching me would bring, but he insisted and eventually won me over.

We weren't as emotionally close as I was with my best friends, but we had our own twisted relationship, focused momentarily on our lustful desires.

I throw on a nightshirt and enter my chambers. Marcus lounges on my bed, still half naked. He's propped on his elbow, watching me alluringly. I can't help but stare at his perfectly sculpted body.

I jump up next to him, and he moves his free arm around me. "Nice fight today," he says.

I roll my eyes. "Kah is a force to be reckoned with, it was pure hatred that made Ryker choose us to fight. I hate him."

"He's a prick, that's what he is."

I nod in agreement.

Marcus rolls over on his back and takes me with him. Pushing myself up, my heart quickens as I find myself straddling him once again.

Resting his hands on my thighs, he grazes his thumbs in circular motions, sending tingles down my body. I begin to slowly move on top of him. Feeling his reaction, I playfully smile. Marcus moves the hem of my nightdress up and rests his hands near my bottom. His brow raise, as he notices I'm not wearing any undergarments.

He pulls my head down and grazes my lips with his. I gently bite down on his bottom lip, making him react even more. He crushes his mouth to mine, and our bodies press firmly together.

Desire radiates between us, as we adjust ourselves and become one. This is exactly what I have been needing. A moan escapes my lips, and I let it push my problems away, allowing myself to only be in this moment.

When we finally succumb to our passion, a thrill runs through the entire length of my body.

Marcus puts his arms around me, and I lean in and kiss him. Our breathing slows and I try to hold onto this serenity before I roll off him and move to his side.

Marcus takes a deep breath. "Have any plans for your birthday?"

I stare into his face. He can't be serious. The corner of his mouth curls up into a smirk.

"Funny." I punch him on the arm.

A knock sounds at the door.

We both bolt up. Marcus cannot be here! I point to beneath my bed, and he jumps down and scrambles underneath. I get down off the bed, and walk slowly to the door, adjusting my nightdress.

On the other side of the door is Bellek. He sweeps past me, and enters my chamber. He looks around swiftly, and turns to face me.

"May I help you?" I ask.

"I just found out about the binding contract. I tried to reason with him. But it's too late. I came to beg you not to do anything rash. It will all work out."

Anger sweeps through me. All I need right now is Marcus. I don't need to be reminded how much my life sucks. Can't I be happy for one second without having someone else confirm my reality?

"I am very aware of my fate, Bellek. I had no other choice but to sign it. And I'll never do anything to jeopardize Zyrik's life, so anything rash is out of the question."

I hear Marcus bump the bed and my heart stops. I pray Bellek hasn't noticed, but it's too late. He cocks his head to the side and his eyes snap to mine. I cower slightly when I see the onset of his rage.

"You play with fire, Vera."

"I don't care."

He steps closer to me, speaking in a low voice.

"Believe me, I want you happy. You deserve happiness, but Marcus is not part of it."

My eyes widen.

Fixing me with his steely grey eyes, he turns and leaves. I hear Marcus drag himself out from under my bed.

"I'd best leave," he mumbles.

I close my eyes. I listen to him gather his things, he rushes by and kisses me on the cheek—then he's gone. I breathe in deeply and slowly let it out. I really can't catch a break.

When nightfall comes, I fall asleep unsure what the morning will bring. As so many times before, I dread waking up to see if my fate is sealed.

5

GOLDEN MIRROR

Midnight comes and goes. Livia and Vera both go to sleep on the eve of their sixteenth birthday, neither knowing if their gift will awaken inside them.

Both of their dreams start off in blackness. Then a tiny bright light starts transforming in the distance, getting brighter and brighter until it comes upon them. Engulfing them.

An explosion of color sparkles all around—whipping around like a soundless wind. When everything settles, a tall golden mirror stands before them.

Not just any golden mirror. But an antique mirror with a gold frame that twists around intricately portrayed details of timeless, ancient, gilded work.

They admire long flowing white gowns that feather down to their feet, disappearing into a fog below. Their long black hair hangs down their backs in soft waves, and each admire her polished look. But it isn't until they see their starkly bright, violet eyes that they see the beauty they now possess.

Stunned by their reflections, one sister brings her hand up to her face but notices her reflection does not mirror her movement. When her eyes shift to what she thinks are her own, she quickly realizes they are someone else's.

Who is this person inside the mirror, someone who is her, yet isn't?

A purple and blue mist gathers around each of them. The golden mirror fades from sight. The mist soaks into their skin and each feel a tingle that covers her entire body, then all ends with a thunderous jolt.

Their dream begins to fade and turns back into darkness. Each is unsure what just happened.

6

LIVIA

MY EYES FLY OPEN. Morning light begins to creep through the canvas flaps. A subtle buzz radiates over me and a strange pulse flows through my veins. The golden mirror, the mist— was it all real?

Throwing my furs off, I rush to the opening, and stumble over our packed supplies.

"Amah!"

Amah rushes over from feeding Rosie.

"En Oli, are you…"

She falters slightly before climbing up and grabbing hold of my face.

"Well, I'll be. It's happened." Her eyes roam over me.

"How can you tell?" I ask.

Amah promptly goes into the back of the wagon. I hear her rummaging around. What is she doing? Finally, she pops back out and hands me her hand mirror. Confused, I take it and peer at my reflection.

"Holy Maker! My eyes!"

"I can no longer deny the prophecy. It's true after all. I never imagined I'd see the magic return. But here it is. My En Oli, a true heir, and a true joy." She takes my hands.

A tingling sensation shoots through me and I jerk my hands back.

"Livia?"

"When you grabbed my hands, I felt something."

Her brow rises. "Try again."

I take her hands hesitantly. This time when the tingling comes, I don't let go. An amused smile lightens Amah's features, and I know she feels something too. Curious, I close my eyes.

My world vanishes. No sound. Only darkness. Amah's hands are luminous in front of me, floating in the air by themselves. I notice the many layers. Her hands are translucent. I see everything.

A red hue pulsates from the joints of her hands. Something pulls me along, pushes to reach out. As if knowing what to do, I sweep the redness away. A golden tint takes its place.

I open my eyes.

Amah inspects her hands, spreading her fingers out in front of her.

"Did you feel it?" I ask.

She nods slowly. "It felt warm, almost hot. Then the feeling vanished, and there was nothing—no warmth, no pain."

"My gift is healing! The gift of Guardian Pynth!"

For so long I've dreamed of this, and now it's my reality.

Amah beams. "Knowing your parents didn't die in vain helps lift some of the sorrow I've carried all these years." She shakes her head in giddy disbelief. "Happy Birthday, En Oli."

She grabs the reins, laughing to herself. This is surreal. Magic is back. And in me!

"I'm glad you decided for us to go to Pynth. I definitely need Regent Grif's protection now. When word gets out, King Kgar will send more than just one assassin after me."

"Yes, he will. We must keep you hidden as best we can until we reach the city. Trust no one."

"Except for Annie. Right?"

"Yes, except for Annie. She'll be as vigilant as I am to make sure you are kept safe."

A light breeze pulls some of my long hair across my face, and I brush it away. Amah once told me that Annie was the only person she could think to take us in those many years ago. They grew up in an orphanage together and always relied on one another. So when Amah escaped with me, she remembered that Annie had moved to Kale. Fortunately, Annie knew of an abandoned cottage out in the pines. For Annie, too, knew the danger I was in.

"Do the people of Pynth know I'm alive?"

"They do. The Regent celebrates your birthday every year in your honor and in hope for your return."

"He does?"

"That's what I've been told."

"Will he and the people expect me to become queen immediately?"

"It's not my place to say. But I've prepared you, so you'll be fine."

"Prepared me? You haven't taught me anything about governing a kingdom."

"I've taught you history."

"History? How can history help me?"

"History is the foundation you need. So you might learn from past mistakes. It's important to learn how the kingdoms trade among themselves. Or learning the different seasons in which our kingdom thrives. Believe it or not, En Oli, but those history lessons will come in very handy when you sit before the council and discuss matters at hand."

I think back to all my boring lessons. That the West relies on Northern furs to get us through our winters, and the North relies on our farming and herbs for their healers.

At the time I couldn't have cared less. I was just a girl in seclusion, far away from the worries of court. We hunted and farmed for ourselves. The items we bought in Kale—I never gave thought to where they came from.

"What about the people?" I ask.

"What do you mean?"

"How am I supposed to rule a people when I've no experience with them?"

"You've been around people."

"Amah. Seriously. All you've ever allowed me to do is sit in the corner of the tavern and watch. You never let anyone speak to me. My people skills are lacking."

"Your skill of reading people will be useful. And talking will come easily enough; you haven't stopped since we left."

My unapologetic scowl makes her laugh. She points up ahead. "Look."

Beyond the trees, a haze of smoke comes curling out from behind a stand of pines in the distance. The town of Kale.

My feet begin their ritual bounce against the foot rail. Soon we will be enjoying the warming comforts of Annie's food.

My all-time favorite dish is crowberry pie. The berries come from the Northern Kingdom, and Annie has them delivered every year for my birthday. I can't wait!

I discovered these small blue berries the same time I discovered walking. A crate of them had just arrived, and Amah set me down for only a moment to help Annie with something. I walked over and stuffed my chubby cheeks with those sweetest of all berries. Annie couldn't even be mad. The blue stains all over my face were punishment enough, and she and Amah still laugh at the memory.

Ever since that day, Annie has made time for this one thing for me on my special day. She cares for me as much as Amah. I know if anything should befall Amah, Annie would be the next best thing.

We come to the first cottage on the outskirts of Kale. Looking past it, cottages dot the snow-covered hills, sitting between trees poking up like jagged green spikes. It's a beautiful scene.

Amah clicks her tongue, speeding Rosie up. As I watch Rosie's slender limbs grace down the road, I can't help but admire how her white coat blends in perfectly with the scenic view.

As we enter the main road into town, not a single mark disturbs the white blanket on the dirt road. With dusk quickly approaching, shops along the road have already closed for the day. It's as if the town has been put to bed, hushed down by the weather and the depleting light.

Bear Horn Inn sits at the end of the road, its perimeters lit a buttery glow from lanterns hung outside between its windows. The inn is three stories, its wood a flawless white pine. Usually the place is busy, but now, on the first day of winter, it seems unusually quiet.

Kale is a diverse village, and people from all over travel through it. Merchants often set up stalls to sell their wares. I loved it when Amah would take me with her to do her shopping. It wasn't often, but those are times I will always remember.

I remember one time when a large caravan came through with brightly colored wagons. They had scarves made of silk and beaded jewelry fit for any young girl who wanted to feel beautiful. One of them being me.

No matter how hard I begged, Amah refused to buy me a single item from the long-haired women. It was the first time I ever thought of running away; I was tired of the tight hold she had on me. Now I understand why she's been so strict.

Amah pulls around in back, where a lantern swings from a barn's entrance. A young boy comes out, the puffs of his breath rushing out like smoke from a chimney.

In a hushed tone, Amah tells me to stay covered. I pull the hood of my cloak over my head and bring it forward slightly to hide my face.

He signals for us to follow him into the large covered barn. Instantly thick walls block the frigid evening air. He unhooks Rosie, then leads her over to some fresh hay and water. He doesn't look familiar and I wonder when Annie hired him on.

When he comes back over, I notice a face covered with freckles and ears too big for his head. He pushes long curly black hair away from his face, and peers up to me.

"Boy, we would like to get inside as soon as possible," Amah says quickly, grabbing his attention. "If you wouldn't mind taking our bags up to a room, we will go on ahead."

"Of course, My Lady."

We leave the stables and cross over a small courtyard to enter the back door of a kitchen, where the aroma of food greets us. My stomach clutches at the rich aromas. A chunk of meat swings back and forth above flames, dripping fat onto a stone hearth.

"My, oh my, look who it is."

My head turns as a heavyset older woman comes bustling in from the front. Annie embraces Amah, and they have a quick exchange of words. Amah leaves promptly, and Annie makes her way over to me--a huge smile spread across her face.

"Livia, my dear."

We fill in the space between us and she wraps her arms around me. She smells of herbs and spices—a comforting aroma. Pushing me back to arm's distance, she takes me in.

"Oh, your eyes! Is it true? For so long I've hoped to see the magic return. And to see it in you? I just know you'll be a great queen."

"Thanks, Annie."

"And don't you worry, you being queen won't stop me from giving you crowberry pie."

She sets pie in front of me, then turns to the chunk of meat hanging from the hearth. She saws off the joint, plops it on a plate, and adds a wedge of cheese to my meal. I waste no time filling my mouth.

By the time Amah comes back, I have already inhaled everything. She proceeds to tell Annie of our encounter with the Silent Watcher while I wait in silence.

"I haven't heard a whisper about intruders. How could he have got past The Wall?"

"I thought the same thing," Amah replies.

"I wonder," Annie continues, "if the Violet Guard is starting to become too relaxed at their posts. I'd mention it to the Regent."

Amah gives a firm nod. "I sent him a message hoping to get an escort within the week. I hope you don't mind our intrusion?"

"Of course I don't mind, you know that. If these assassins are getting through, I would rather have the two of you here rather than out there alone." Annie shifts in her chair. "I'm not supposed to say this, but I think it might help put your mind at ease. The Regent's right-hand man is here. He arrived four days ago."

Amah straightens up. "What's he doing here?"

"His mother passed away a couple of weeks ago, up north. He came by to collect his brother and they are just passing through to go back to the city. You met his brother only moments ago—the young boy in the stable. He loves horses, and his brother asked if he could help. I couldn't say no."

A pang sweeps through my chest. How awful.

"If you want, I can let him know you are here?"

"I'll think on it," Amah replies. "Thank you."

After a few more pleasantries, Annie takes us to our room.

We find comfort in the softness of our beds before I fall asleep. I can only hope these next few days fly by fast.

I AWAKE SOMETIME in the night, startled by a disturbing dream. Turning on my side to face Amah, I discover her gone. I often wonder if she ever sleeps at all.

No longer tired, I go to the window. The silver moon is high in the sky giving off the only light shining over the quiet town. Before long, I'll be in my own city, finally getting to experience my own form of community. Every time I think of it, a thrill of excitement courses through me. And to know I have the gift?

A movement down the street catches my attention. A large man steps out from the shadows. My blood turns ice cold. He's the size of the assassin I saw two days ago. An alarm goes off inside me. I must warn Amah.

Pulling on my trousers and boots, I grab my cloak and rush out the door and down the stairs. The tavern is dark and empty. Staying in the shadows of the room, I keep clear of the moonbeams that cast light across the floor. Through the window, I see the Silent Watcher move toward the back of the house.

Dashing through the kitchens, I open the back door. A soft glow comes from the barn and I rush towards them in hopes of finding Amah.

Instead, I find the boy from earlier, brushing Rosie down. He has no idea what danger lurks around the corner.

Not having much time, I hurry to his side. He startles when he sees me, and I press my finger to my lips. His eyes widen but he keeps quiet.

Whispering as softly as I can, I tell him that we need to hide. I point to the covered wagon and we both quickly climb inside.

The assassin steps out from the shadows. I'm unsure if he's seen us. All I can make out is his large frame.

I feel the boy shaking next to me, and I reach over to calm him. Despair flashes through me. This boy's pain feels deep.

He covers his mouth, and I'm sure he felt my gift. But when his pale face looks over my shoulder, I look back to the assassin's silhouette up against the canvas. All he has left to do is peer behind the loose flap, to see both of us sitting inside.

I frantically look around for something I can use to defend us, when I hear the ring of another blade drawn.

"Are you lost, assassin?" It's a man's voice.

A second blade is drawn. Taking a chance, I creep forward and peek through the gap. I can't see the man who spoke because the bulk of the assassin fills my view.

The assassin attacks. The challenger sidesteps and blocks him—he's probably hoping to get him away from us. But then again, does he know we are here?

The assassin advances again and the man pivots back, blocking his blade a second time. Footsteps approach from behind them and I instantly recognize Amah's gait.

The assassin swipes his blade towards Amah. Horror fills my chest. I scream out.

Amah's sword comes up to meet his and they turn to see my head poking out from behind the flap.

Aggression from the assassin comes full force. Amah and the challenger meet his advance, determined to keep him from me.

"Grab horses, and go!" The man yells.

Amah drops back and hurries over to me.

"Quick Livia, get on Rosie. I'll grab another horse. Hurry!"

"But Amah..."

"No time to discuss. Go!"

Reaching back, I grab the boy and pull him forward. I

can't leave him behind. Amah's lips press firmly together seeing my dilemma.

"I'll take him with me. Now go."

I climb out from the back and hurry to Rosie. In no time, we are riding swiftly out into the night, escaping the night's sudden terror. I can only hope the stranger has our same luck.

7

VERA

A BRILLIANT SHADE of violet looks at me from my reflection. I should be excited. But I'm not.

I'd awakened in a pool of my own sweat, terrified of what I would see. So now, as I look at my reflection, it reminds me of the binding contract, of the noose tight around my neck.

Everyone will know of the change by looking at me. What they won't know, is that a strange hum encompasses my body, forcing it to cooperate. I'm curious to know what gift this might be. So, too, will the king.

I dress quickly, suppressing this new sensation. It won't be long before the king learns my eyes have changed. Until then I'll enjoy what time I have left.

My first stop of the morning takes me to Zyrik. I peek my head inside and see his bed empty. My first instinct is to panic, thinking the king has taken him. But I remain calm and step further inside. Zyrik suddenly jumps out from behind a chair, throwing small pieces of paper in the air. Relief escapes my lungs in a burst.

Zyrik runs towards me and jumps into my arms, squeezing his arms around my neck.

"Hey, you!"

He pulls back to look at me. Fear takes hold of him and he wiggles out from my embrace and retreats to the back of the room.

"It's okay, Little Rik. It's still me. I got different colored eyes for my birthday. Do you like them?" I turn my head side to side.

Zyrik squints, his tongue slightly pushed out. Seconds later, he comes running back.

"Oh, you are getting so big."

He puts his hands on either side of my face and peers into my eyes. He moves my head in small movements, looking from every angle.

"Do you like them?"

Zyrik shrugs his shoulders.

"Yeah, me too." He releases my face. "So, what are you doing today? Anything exciting?"

He points over to his chest of toys.

"That seems like fun."

He nods and smiles. He points to me, then to himself, before motioning over to the chest.

"I wish I could stay and play, I really do. But I'm going to be extra busy today. But, I promise I'll come see you later. You must promise me that you'll stay out of trouble."

His blonde curls bounce as he makes a crisscross over his heart with a finger. Kissing him on the cheek, I let him go.

How I wish I could stay with him, away from what the rest of this day will entail. Unfortunately, I can't hide so easily. Especially from the king and his dumb councilmen.

ALREADY THE CASTLE IS AWAKE, and busy with the final touches for my birthday celebration. Curious eyes find me, and I duck my head. I just need a little bit longer to enjoy this day without them wagging their tongues.

I pass through the stables and look up to the arena. I sigh.

The biggest challenge will be avoiding thousands of assassins. If only I could wear a mask. Wisps of white clouds form neat lines above, dragged by a wind I can't feel.

Halfway up the hill, a shout disturbs my thoughts.

"Vera, wait!"

Nate, Karl, and Murrow are running to catch up. They must've just completed a shift. They are dressed out in their black threads and leather armor, all of them holding their red masks. Then it dawns on me.

Today is also the day for The Silent Trials. Which means not only do I have to avoid thousands of assassins, but also the king and the people of Dryden.

My mood plummets.

Nate is the first to see my expression. "You forgot..." He stops mid sentence on seeing my eyes, while Karl and Murrow groan as they lag behind.

"You know, Vera, it's not that hard to remember," Murrow blurts out.

Karl punches him in the arm. "Easy Murrow, or you might find something important cut off one day."

"Yeah, right!"

They finally catch up and notice Nate's silence. Both finally look at me, and their mouths fall open.

"Wicked."

"Does this mean you have the gift?" Karl asks.

"I'm not sure what the gift is yet. But I'm sure if I don't find out soon, the king will torture it out of me."

We continue to walk towards Graves Hill. They wish me a happy birthday and don't say any more about my gift. I'm glad they don't make a big deal about it; it's one of the many reasons they've been my friends this long—they know when to shut up. Instead, I fill them in on the contract I signed.

"It's not right," Karl grumbles. He runs his hand through his ash brown hair, but it falls right back over his protruding brow.

"It's beyond not right. You know how many times we've planned the king's death?" Murrow complains.

It's true. We've spent many evenings contemplating hundreds of different ways to kill the king. We even all agreed that I would be the one to give the final blow. So much for wishing.

I take note of Nate's silence. "What's wrong with you?"

He shakes his head and frowns. Kicking a rock off the path, he finally answers. "How much longer do you have to suffer, Vera? I hate all this, and you deserve so much more."

I remember when Nate first arrived at Graves Hill. He'd been ripped from his family at the ripe age of eight and forced to become an assassin. He later found out his parents were killed for trying to stop his abduction. I was the one who comforted him when he couldn't function during our training. I shared my own story and told him we had to do what they wanted to survive. We have been best friends ever since.

My throat clenches. "Thanks, Nate."

We hear the sound of the drums starting as we enter the arena. Today everyone will be dressed out and wearing red masks. There is nothing more daunting then a force of uniformed Silent Watchers. This is why the people fear them.

In the center, ten whipping blocks are lined up along a wooden stage. Two assassins paces back and forth, holding the whips they will use to inflict pain. Just by the arrogant struts of one of them, I know it is Kah. Bastard. Not only is he to be exempt, but he is ruthless with just the flick of his wrist.

It's lucky for me it's my birthday. So I, too, am exempt. King Kgar likes me healthy for the evening's celebration.

"Where are you guys today?"

"Not the cages, thank the Maker." Murrow says in relief.

Murrow and the others slide their masks on. I wave goodbye as we go our separate ways.

The Silent Trials follow the same rules as on any other day. Except that for today, it's a tournament. The assassins have been split up amongst all the different stations. You don't want to be assigned to the cages.

Today, the cages can seal one's fate to the mines. Ten sparring cages have been built in front of the king's platform. If you lose, the king decides your fate—a whipping block or the mines. No one wants to go to the mines.

This whole event is entertainment for the people. King Kgar knows he must give something to them. This is how he does it. Bets will be made, and coin will flow at a cost to the participants.

I run for the furthest cage, away from the king and his ever watchful Woman of the Scree. My stomach tightens as I see those two in the stands. Fortunately, they haven't seen me—yet.

Captain Leech stands inside a cage and is already choosing the first two fighters. Unlike Ryker, his matchups aren't out of spite. The drums cease beating, casting silence over the entire arena.

Bellek steps onto the whipping block stage, his red commander cloak demanding our attention.

"Let The Silent Trials begin!"

The crowd roars and the wagers are offered.

HOURS PASS by with fight after fight. Most losers go to the whipping block, but it's worse for those few sent to the mines. I watch as an assassin hands over his red mask and then steps into the back of a wagon, one that will take him straight to the mines in Wolfmere Peaks.

All of our lives we've been taught to not fear the Peaks, but old stories circle around. All of us know about the magical creatures that once lurked in the mountains. Rumor says nothing has been seen of them since the magic was taken. But some claim to have seen monstrous shadows at dusk that resemble nightmares. With our mines located at the edge of Wolfmere Peaks, we never know who makes it to the mines. We do know that not everyone returns.

"Slyk and Marcus!"

My eyes snap into focus hearing Marcus's name. With everyone wearing masks I wasn't aware he was around.

My heart thumps hard inside my chest. Not from nerves, but from the thrill of seeing him fight. Marcus is one of our top fighters. His skills are what drew me to him to begin with.

Slyk is another one of Captain Ryker's cronies. His slim frame and elongated neck give him the impression of a weasel. Marcus towers over him, flexing his arms. As always, overly arrogant.

Captain Leech signals them to start. Marcus immediately goes for Slyk's legs. Slyk is ready and pivots back, coming down hard with his elbow, aiming for Marcus's back. Whipping around, Marcus catches Slyk's elbow and punches him hard in his face.

They fight hard for long minutes, neither one weakening. Eventually, they both end up on the ground. Slyk wraps his legs around Marcus, pinning him in place. Each time Slyk throws a punch, Marcus blocks him. Soon enough you can sense Slyk's frustration.

Marcus thrusts his hips up hard causing Slyk to loosen enough for him to escape. They scramble around, sand flying everywhere. Each tries to get a grip on the other. Suddenly, Marcus gets a hold of Slyk's arm and pulls it between his legs and falls back. A loud pop is heard. Slyk yells out in pain.

Captain Leech calls the fight. Marcus drags himself up, exhaustion marked in his heavy breathing. He turns to exit the cage, leaving Slyk to cradle his arm.

But Slyk makes a movement that I can't ignore. A flash of silver comes up in his good hand. He wasn't supposed to have any weapons on him! Panicked, I look to Marcus who has no idea his life is in danger.

I imagine Slyk's arm breaking in half. At the same time, I

throw a knife of my own. A pained cry escapes his lips as I watch his arm snap in half, his bone popping out through the skin. As this unfolds, my knife pierces his eye.

The assassins around me take a step back, exposing me for my crime. The audience, however, sees entertainment and their cheers only get louder. My problem now is I'm in full view of King Kgar, and I'm sure he has witnessed everything. Including the use of my gift.

A messenger is sent to determine my fate.

Slyk's body lays lifeless. His arm is a mangled mess. Marcus stands outside the cage. He shakes his head. The men around me start to fidget, having witnessed something they have never seen before. I too am unsure what to think.

The messenger finally comes back and delivers the word to Captain Leech. I wait. Leech turns and twirls his hand in the air.

I'm yanked by my collar by rough hands that couldn't care less about being subtle. I look to the king. His face has no expression as his dark gaze locks on mine. Unable to keep my balance, my feet stumble over themselves as I'm dragged to the whipping block. Kah grabs me from the Watcher and throws me up against a post. He straps my hands up to the metal ring, then unhooks my bodice in back. A knife slices through my black threads. Punishment is to be on bare skin.

I know the lashes will flay my back open, and my body slightly trembles at the thought. But I hold my head up high, too proud to let them sense my fear. If this is what the king wants, then this is what he will get.

Kah grabs his whip and smooths it out. Even with his red mask on, I sense his smirk. I skim the crowd and my eyes fall on an assassin wearing a red cloak—the Commander. Will he save me?

Goosebumps form over my entire body with my skin suddenly exposed. Holding my breath, I brace myself for the oncoming pain.

Crack. I grit my teeth, biting down on the sharp pain. I keep my head held high.

Crack. Crack. My body arches and warm blood travels down my back.

Crack. I scream. The lash hits across my ribs, the sting shoots through my body. As the lashes continue, tears escape down my face. I can't control them.

Crack. My legs finally give out and my back is on fire.

Crack. Crack. Small black dots fill my vision.

After the last three lashes are given—my world turns to darkness.

I WISH I WERE DEAD. It would be better than having the fire of pain covering my back. Trying to gather my senses, I become aware of a bubbling up of water. I open my eyes. The Scree's head is bobbing above a pool of water. The bath house, I realize. It's where all the assassins come to bathe. The cave is near Graves Hill, built around a hot springs.

The Scree's mouth curves up into a sly grin.

"Vera, Vera. A girl who can sure make an entrance. Did you know that I felt your gift the moment you used it?"

I don't respond.

"Yes, it was quite a lovely thrill. It didn't surprise me that your first time using it would end up killing someone. I always knew you were a vicious little vixen. And to protect a boy?"

I refuse to take her bait.

The Scree laughs. "Oh Vera, I can smell him on you. To be honest, I'm a bit disappointed. I was sure your lover would be the tall blond I saw you entering the arena with earlier. Now *he* is an attractive assassin, hmm?"

Anger rolls through me—stupid bitch.

The Scree glides through the water, coming over to the edge where I am lying. If the pain weren't so paralyzing, I would move away. She slowly stands and I see that she is naked. Unable to move my head away, I close my eyes—it doesn't help. The image of her perfect breasts and tiny waist are imprinted inside my head.

I flinch when she touches my back.

"What the hell are you doing? Get off me!"

"Shhh. This will only take a second."

The pain begins to fade and I realize she's using the Enchanter's magic. The king must've sent her to put me back together. He knew this lashing would put me out for days. Yet he allowed it to happen.

Her hands retract and she splashes back into the spring. I open my eyes. With my pain now at a dull ache, I push myself up. I too am naked. I slide into the spring, trying to hide my flawed body from the Scree—but she's already seen it.

"The Enchanter could fix those grotesque scars of yours. For a small price, of course."

I ignore her jab and wade away from her, moving towards the opening of the cave. I have no interest in entertaining her, or accidentally spilling anything that could get my friends in trouble. The Scree is a creation of the Enchanter. She has zero empathy for human life. She lives only for the Enchanter, and I have no desire to let him into any of my world.

"You know, your gift is interesting. Did you know it's the gift from the North?"

I pause.

"Your mother was from the North. Oh! You never knew your mother did you?"

I swallow a lump that forms in my throat. She knows very well I never knew my parents. Because of her magic-hoarding master and his stupid prophecy, I never got the chance to have a family.

Done with her torturous conversation, I jump out from the springs, and run out—not caring that I am naked.

. . .

ENTERING MY CHAMBER, I see a package lying on my bed. It's from the king, as is such a package every year.

Opening it, I find a beautiful white gown folded neatly inside. I lift it up. Tiny diamonds are scattered over the entire gown. I let the satin fabric drop down to the floor, revealing intricate designs.

The fabric alone must've cost a fortune. It has to have come from the North. That's where all the expensive fabrics come from— silk and satin in particular. I think back to what the Scree had said. My gift is the Northern magic—Northern like my mother. I shake my head, pushing away the sadness that tries to surface.

I step into the gown and pull it up around my neck. I step in front of my mirror. It is truly the most beautiful gown I've ever seen. The dipping neckline shows off parts of me in a way that makes me look stunning. I look like someone else entirely.

I turn around and look over my shoulder, pulling my hair aside. My skin screams red. Ugly welts overlap one another— a reminder of the stupidity of my decisions. The Scree could've made them disappear in her healing, but she stopped short on purpose. She loves control.

I spend the next hour soaking in the tub, letting my hair hang over the edge to dry. I still can't believe I was able to do that to Slyk. I might not have been excited about my gift earlier, but the reality of what I can do is quite invigorating. If I concentrate, I can still feel the subtle hum over my skin.

I'm surprised I don't have the gift of healing. It's what the West usually inherits from their Guardian—at least they did centuries ago. And as far as I knew before, I was from the West.

A knock comes at my chamber door. *Great*. The chamber-maids have arrived. I am instantly annoyed.

Every year the king sends these maids to gloss me over for the evening. They paint my face, fashion my hair in the latest style, and powder my body in glitter. It's embarrassing. The assassins who get a glimpse of me, they rag on me the whole next week.

I dry myself off and answer the door.

"I'm all yours."

They rush past me, and the giggling starts. I grit my teeth and do my best to shut them out. Let the torture begin.

I walk carefully down the corridor, trying not to trip over my gown. The chambermaids decided to leave half of my hair down in hopes of covering the fresh marks across my back. A hush went through the room when the chambermaids first removed my garments. You would think they'd be used to my scarred body by now. But each year, it's the same.

Bellek is waiting for me at the end of the hall. As always, when he sees me all dressed up on my birthday, he bows.

This time, I curtsy.

"Wow. A true lady!" He pulls a wooden box out from behind his back and hands it to me. "Happy Birthday, Vera."

I hesitantly take the box. He has never given me a gift before. I unlatch the lid and open it.

Lying inside is a warrior's necklace. Hanging from a large knot on a leather cord, are three small grey stones and a feather from a Kepper, our most feared bird of prey.

"It's beautiful!" I gently caress the red feather.

A Kepper is a dangerous beast that can easily rip you to shreds with its razor sharp talons. But they are beautiful birds, red with black masks that extend to their beaks. To capture just one feather speaks volumes about the type of warrior you are.

"I knew from the moment you were able to walk that you would be a warrior," he says. "You might not go out to fight in battles, but the true battle is inside this place and inside yourself. These are battles just the same. I've watched you become a strong and fearless young woman, and I'm proud of you."

His words touch deep. The love and respect I have for him is real and I wouldn't be who I am without him. I wish I could embrace him this once, but I've already pushed the limits for one day.

"Thanks, Bellek. Your gift couldn't be more perfect. Do you think I might get one more thing from you?"

His brow raises in question.

"Walk with me to my party?"

If I am going to spend time with a bunch of rich kiss-ups, I can think of no one better to go in with.

8

LIVIA

WE RODE for hours until Amah decided there was enough distance between us and the threat. In our escape, Amah had thrown the boy on a horse of his own. He has now drifted away a short distance, keeping to himself.

His name is Oliver. The man fighting the assassin and who helped us escape was his brother.

"Livia, quit staring."

"But I feel bad for him. He doesn't even know if his brother is okay or not. I feel like there is something I should do for him."

"Well, don't. Leave him be."

I pull my cloak tight around my shoulders. The ground is still covered with a thin layer of snow, tufts of grass poking out in random places. But the chill in the air warns us of more snow.

I glance over and Oliver is whispering to his horse.

"Aren't we more interesting than a horse?"

Amah breathes out heavily from her nose. I can tell I'm testing her patience.

"He's just lost his mother, and he has no idea what has happened to his brother. Let him find comfort in his horse.

Besides, we don't need him poking around and asking questions. The less he knows, the better."

What is he going to do? Tell the trees? I keep the sarcastic comments to myself. They would only irritate her more.

"I want to point out the bad decision you made to leave your bed. You should've stayed there."

"But I didn't know where you were! And I saw the Silent Watcher. What was I supposed to do?" I shake my head. "You know I can't just stand by, and do nothing. And when I came across Oliver, I couldn't leave his fate to the assassin. I'm no monster."

A silence stretches between us.

"I should never have left you," she says.

"Why? Because you think me weak?"

"That's not what I meant."

"I told you, I'm not queen material."

Amah pinches the bridge of her nose.

"Livia. Your actions alone make you queen material. Sacrificing yourself to protect others is the number one quality a successful ruler must have. I said I should never have left you, because what you lack is the skill to protect yourself."

"Oh."

"I'm sorry for not being there. However, this whole situation shows me how brave you are. I'm proud of you—as would be your parents."

"Thanks," I say. "I like to think I would make them proud."

"And En Oli?"

"Yes?"

"You are definitely queen material."

I smile awkwardly as a heavy weight of responsibility settles into my stomach. I still don't understand why a kingdom would want a sixteen-year-old to rule over them.

"How old was Queen Bellflower when she first became queen?"

"I'm not sure. The Temple will have plenty of material for you to scour through. I'm sure you will find all your answers there."

"Temple? Pynth's Temple in Willow Round?"

"That's the one."

"Weren't you raised there?"

"For a time."

"Oh! Isn't the undying Willow there, too."

She rolls her eyes at my excitement. She knows I love to talk about anything to do with magic. The undying Willow has stood for thousands of years. It is no longer in bloom now that magic is gone, but surprisingly enough, it remains upright and has yet to wither away. The idea of seeing it in person is fascinating. We can't get there fast enough.

We stop for a short break, and lead our horses over to a patch of grass near the edge of the pines. Amah sends Oliver and me out in a search for anything that we can eat. In our rush to escape, we were unable to grab any of our packs.

Now that I think of it, these next two days will be miserable without any of our supplies. We can only hope that Oliver's brother will catch up to us shortly; or the Regent's guard will find us soon.

Twigs and pine needles crunch loudly under Oliver's boots. I can tell he's never spent time in the woods. My feet know how to glide quietly over the forest floor. It took me years of practice not to raise an alarm to anything we might be hunting. Which reminds me of something else we left behind—my bow.

I follow after Oliver, hoping to give him some friendly advice on what to look for. As I approach, he wipes his face.

Sadness settles over me seeing the tears he sheds. I reach out and he flinches, surprised by my closeness. His red-rimmed eyes scrunch together and I do the only thing I can think of—I embrace him.

"I'm sorry about your mother." I whisper softly in his ear.

His body slumps and he trembles in my arms. The hum of my gift comes to surface. This time, I know what to do.

I close my eyes.

He stands in front of a black background. Instead of a red hue, however, the color blue radiates off his body. I can't stop myself from feeling the despair that plagues his heart.

I can't just push this away. My gut feeling tells me to pull the blue into myself. I gently flow my gift out and let my comfort transfer over to him. At the same time, I pull the blue inside myself.

His inner strength becomes stronger.

I open my eyes.

"What did you just do to me?" he chokes out.

"Nothing," I lie. "I just thought you might need a hug."

"No, I felt what you did. I know you have the gift. It's why your eyes are that way."

So he does know. A brightness appears in his eyes and a smile spreads across his face. "I felt my sadness fade, and for once I can breathe. Thank you."

I tuck my hair behind my ear. "I just wanted to help you."

"Are you the princess our kingdom has been waiting for?"

I nod.

Amah yells after us—her tone alarming. Not caring to keep quiet, we dash quickly back to where she and the horses were resting.

Amah is standing at the edge of the pines, pacing back and forth. When she sees us, she motions us to be quick.

A deep rumbling moves under our feet. Looking over her shoulder, three black cloaked riders are traveling fast and heading our way.

"Who are they?" I ask.

"Silent Watchers." She hurries me over to Rosie, as Oliver steps back into the trees.

"I want you to listen to me very closely. When they get here, they will dismount. The moment I say go, you mount

up and ride hard south. I'll hold them off for as long as I can."
I shake my head. "Look, I know what you're thinking. But we can't let them have you. You are the rightful queen and our people need you. You can't think of me."

Amah reaches up and wipes a tear that escapes down my face. We both know she will not survive this attack.

"Can I take Oliver?"

Amah shakes her head. "He will only add weight to Rosie. We need her to fly like the wind. I'm sorry, En Oli."

I glance to Oliver. "He could be a diversion. Put him on his own horse and have him go north."

Amah agrees and tells Oliver the plan. To ensure they can't surround us, we stand at the edge of the pines.

The assassins stop a few paces from us. As Amah predicted, they dismount and stalk our way.

Their red masks are frightening and I can't stop the tremble in my legs. Any of the three of them could take us down without a thought. I can only imagine what they are thinking, seeing an old woman, a girl, and a young boy in front of them. I'm surprised they aren't laughing.

Amah pulls her sword out. "Go!"

Many things happen at once. Oliver and I run to our horses and mount quickly. Amah rushes the three assassins with a war-like yell and I kick my heels in as she swings her blade.

Fear grips me as Rosie takes off. This could be the last time I ever see Amah. My stomach knots up as I sneak a quick look back. Instead of seeing Amah, I see an assassin on his horse following after me.

I dig in deeper with my heels. Rosie's ears prick back, and she swiftly tears through the snow. My knuckles are white from clenching the reins tightly, fearing if I loosen my grip at all, I might fall.

Following along the narrow strip of trail, snow flings out

behind me, and I know it won't be long before the assassin catches up.

Taking another chance, I glance back again. The Silent Watcher is right on top of me. I jerk the reins to the left as he comes up close on my right. The motion doesn't shake him and he reaches out and grabs hold of my reins. I hit his hands, trying to get him to loosen his grip, but he doesn't budge.

He pulls up on my reins and brings us out from our full-on gallop. I'm still hitting at his hands when he grabs my hand and twists it. Pain shoots down my arm as he rips me from my horse and drags me over to his. I'm fighting with all the strength I can muster, when something heavy hits me over the head. Blackness takes hold of me.

UGH. A wave of nausea rolls through my body. Already I feel the lump on my head. Groggily, I open my eyes and my world is flashing by. A deep throb pounds inside my head as I try to gather what's left of my senses.

A gust of wind hits my face. As I attempt to push back my hair, I realize my hands are tied down to the horn of the saddle. Monstrous arms hold on to the reins on either side of me; my eyes follow up them. A red mask greets me and I quickly turn away. I twist my wrists, but there's no give to allow me to loosen the knot.

With my body flush up against his chest, it leaves me no room to look around. I'm unsure if he's continuing south. I would guess not, seeing as he's from the East.

A low rumble comes from behind us and the assassin tenses. Suddenly, I'm pushed forward as the Silent Watcher digs into the horse's side to push us faster. Wet snow flies in the air, and I find myself dodging a cold spray of ice.

I attempt to look behind, but the assassin's too big. As the rumble grows louder it reminds me of a thunderstorm creeping up to our door. I can only hope that whoever is chasing us, is on my side.

The Silent Watcher jerks the horse to the right, sending us into dense trees. Small branches smack across my face, leaving cuts on my skin. The forest floor has patches of rocky terrain and the assassin maneuvers around them. One wrong move could be deadly.

I catch a movement to my right. I can barely make out a dozen cloaked riders. My chest expands, feeling a sense of relief. None of them are wearing red masks; it gives me the hope I need.

An arrow whizzes close by, zipping past my ear. Bless the Maker! Who are they shooting at! My heart thuds inside my chest, reacting to the sudden danger. More riders gallop past us, making escape impossible on our current path.

The Silent Watcher suddenly slams against me and tumbles off the horse. With only a second to look back, I see an arrow protruding from his neck. I try not to panic. With the assassin no longer guiding the horse, I'm now being carried by an out-of-control steed.

The horse tears through the woods, taking its own unreliable path. It doesn't care where it takes me.

Twisting my wrists, I try to grab hold of the reins as if my life depends on it. The jostle from the horse keeps me from staying upright in the saddle and I slowly begin to slide sideways. At the rate we're going, any type of contact could kill me.

A tree up ahead has a broken branch jutting out into our path. If my horse doesn't adjust soon, it doesn't look good for me. Riders ahead try to block the treacherous path. But my horse continues straight for the branch. I clench my eyes tight and await the impact. Suddenly, my horse jerks to the side.

My eyes flash open to see a rider grabbing hold of the horse's reins. He slows us down until we stop. Instantly a burning pain erupts around my wrists.

The rider pulls back his hood, revealing a mess of tousled brown hair that curls out from under his ears. His strong rugged features are full of concern as he unsheathes his knife and begins cutting away the rope that binds my wrists.

I can't help but notice how long his eyelashes are, reaching down to the arch of his cheek. A long thin scar runs along his left side of his jaw, and I find myself suddenly interested in how he got it.

When the last thread of rope is cut away, I begin massaging my wrists; soreness is already running deep.

"Thank you."

He doesn't respond, but sits there and stares at me with the most curious expression. There's an intensity and a gentleness to be found in the depth of this rider's blue eyes, and a warmth spreads through my chest as he continues to look at me. Is he observing me the same way I am him?

"Your Royal Highness, I am Reddik."

I freeze. I recognize the sound of his voice.

"Do I know you?"

"We haven't formally met. But yes, My Lady, I was the one back in Kale."

"Oh!" An alarm rings in my head. "Oliver! He's your brother! He was heading back to Kale to help with my escape. Did you see him?" Worry snakes through me, and I can't control the drumming of my heart.

Reddik shut his eyes and breathes in deep.

"He was being chased by a Silent Watcher when I discovered him. He's been badly injured."

I shake my head, fighting back tears.

"But is he alive? Is he okay?"

Sadness clouds his features. "He's alive, but only barely."

Relief courses through me.

"Then we must hurry to him. There is no time to waste."

"There's no use, My Lady. Nothing can save him."

"I can."

9

VERA

"The color of your eyes reminds me of stories I heard as a child."

"Really?" We descend the stairs near the Great Hall.

"Each kingdom was known by the color of their ruler's eyes, a color passed down from the Guardians themselves. Not very many people now believe it, but they will once they see yours."

"The Scree said my gift came from the North. Are Guardian Icewyn's eyes violet?"

Bellek purses his lips. "No. Your eyes come from Guardian Pynth."

"What are the colors of the other kingdoms?" I ask.

"Guardian Dryden has light grey, almost white eyes. Guardian Acadia's are red, and Guardian Icewyn's are ice blue."

I try to imagine a crowd of people with those colors. Would I be around to see all the magic unfold? There are so many other questions I want to ask, but I dare not.

We finally reach the grand staircase that leads down into the Great Hall. The room is covered in gilded gold, and hundreds of guests are dressed in the brightest of colors. The room's warm, and the quantity of food and drink could feed a village.

Music drifts into the air; festive beats have the people dancing. It's a spectacle that I have to endure once a year with people who couldn't care less about me.

Bellek stays a step behind me as we descend into the crowd. A servant hands me a glass of wine. I've never tasted wine before, and I drink it quickly. A sweetness, mixed with a bitter tang, coats my tongue. Not sure if I like it, I take another.

Bellek retrieves it from my hand.

"Easy, Vera. This wine will knock you off your feet if you're not careful." Already a lightness settles over me.

Walking further in, people begin to recognize me. They stare openly. It's awkward how they treat me, as if I'm not human. I so badly want to scream at them. But it's pointless.

Their unabashed gawking doesn't surprise me. I've always been something to look at but never someone for them to get to know. Some of these people only see me on this one day—a spectacle they pay money for.

I move past them and observe the dancing. Faces are flush with a giddiness that shows me wine has been flowing freely this night.

The women's dresses are beautiful, and complement their smooth skin. It's a presentation of beauty I'll never achieve. I hate my flaws.

The king's chair at the high table is empty, and the large curtain hanging behind it is peculiar. I've never seen it there before. What could he possibly be revealing aside from me?

"It's her!"

A nobleman with a large hooked nose who resembles a bird is pointing at me. His cheeks are red from his drink, and his eyes are bright. He looks me up and down, his mouth curling up in a leer.

A subtle hum spreads across the surface of my skin. My

gift doesn't seem to enjoy his staring. His lips part to speak, but he remains silent. He knows he can't make a comment about me—the punishment would be instant death.

The doors across the room open, revealing the king. The crowd cheers, and I try to hide my disgust for these people who would cheer a man like him.

Bruce marches in behind him, his eyes roaming over the crowd. The humming over my body intensifies. I allow my gift to touch his heart. His eyes widen. I could kill him now if I so dared.

The room quiets when they reach the high table. Where's the Scree? I glance around, but she's nowhere to be seen.

"Welcome, councilmen, and people of the court!" Another round of applause goes around. "And welcome, of course, to our dear birthday girl, Vera!"

Everyone turns to me, clapping as if they care. I know better. King Kgar sweeps out his arms, motioning me to come forward. Leaving Bellek's side, I saunter my way up next to the king.

The gleam in his eyes sends a shiver down my spine. I know what he visualizes, seeing me in this dress. It's sickening.

"You look ravishing, my dear. It's perfect on this special day, isn't it? It hurt my feelings that you didn't share your wonderful news with me. Finding out after others? Tsk, tsk." He faces the crowd, leaving me feeling uneasy with what is to inevitably come.

"I'm pleased to announce that our long wait for magic to return has finally ended. Vera has been blessed by the Maker himself. She will now represent our kingdom and bring forth victories in my name."

An excited chatter fills the hall. They know their pockets will grow heavier when distant kingdoms are conquered.

"In honor of this glorious occasion, I've planned some

entertainment." The Woman of the Scree comes out from behind the curtain, and releases the drapes.

There is always that one button that sends me into a blind fury. Zyrik. Seeing him in a cage dressed as a court jester pushes that button.

When Zyrik notices the crowd, he curls up in the back of the cage and sticks his thumb in his mouth. I can tell he's already been crying.

Anger blazes through me. Glaring at the king, he has the audacity to grin. "You should've come to me when you discovered your gift," he whispers. "This, my dear, is your punishment."

He straightens and turns to address the crowd. My heart thumps hard in my chest. "Who here wants to have the king's own jester in their home? We all know what a joke he has been from the moment he was born."

The crowd laughs. Everyone knows the king has denounced him as an heir. A weakling, saved by the kidnapped princess—both of them misfits.

Immediately bids are placed amongst the crowd. The nobleman resembling the bird, laughs and points, raising his hand, playing along with the king's game.

My emotions rise and I ignite my gift fully, muting from my ears the sounds of the room. Is this what the king wants? Does he want to humiliate his son in front of me to punish me, or to bring forth my gift? Either way, if he wants a show, I will give it to him.

An electricity sparks over my body. Unlike before, when I didn't know what I was doing, I take pause and embrace what the gift guides me to do.

When those in front see my expression, their smiles fade. But for them it's too late. With a single thought, I send them to their knees. A unified thud echoes throughout the hall followed by cries and shouts of fury, mixed with fear.

They look at me, dumbstruck, no longer seeing me as a

useless accessory, but as someone who has just brought forth something powerful. A few are even stupid enough to laugh, probably thinking the king has me under control. Oh, how they are wrong.

I am beyond angry and past the point of caring. Humiliating me is one thing, but doing it to Zyrik is something else entirely—he's my life. The king steps up behind me. "Kill one. Show me what you can do."

I walk down to the bird-like man and force him up with only a thought. His nostrils flare and sweat beads his brow. He's obviously frightened now that he's fully aware of what I can do. His eyes plead with me but I push my guilt aside. I have to do this. I wrap my gift around his heart and squeeze it tight—he drops dead to the floor. The crowd screams.

10

LIVIA

A TROOP of the Violet Guard is gathered around the back of two large wagons, each bearing a willow emblem. Reddik jumps off his horse but before he can help me, I'm already dismounting. My boots hit the ground and I run towards the center of the men, pushing them aside.

Stepping past the last man, I see Amah, who has somehow survived, kneeling next to Oliver. He's lying motionless in a pool of his own blood.

Reddik brushes past me and kneels at his brother's side. Amah and I exchange looks; with relief also comes worry. Oliver doesn't look good. He's lost so much blood.

I go to his other side, take the hand that's covering his wound, and move it gently to his side. The gash is deep.

I close my eyes, and silence falls. The pulse of my own heartbeat echoes in my ears, but the boy's pulse is barely thumping. I can feel cold creeping over his body.

I push my gift over him. Along with his deep wound, his wrist is also broken. I bring the torn pieces of his belly back together first, mending up to the surface of his skin, and smoothing out the jagged edges. The organs are next. Each graze and cut disappears, and lost blood replenishes.

I turn my attention to his wrist. Without even thinking of how to piece together the shattered bone, my gift whirls around it, putting everything back in place.

A warmth spreads over me and I open my eyes. Sharp pain greets me, shooting across my head. I try to push it away as Oliver attempts to sit up.

"Whoa. Easy." Reddik puts his hand behind Oliver's back and helps guide him up. He shakes his head in disbelief.

When I look around, the guards are gawking at me. The magic that has been gone for a century is back. Each and every guard bends his knee and bows his head.

I sneak a glance to Amah. Her face glows with pride. Unable to hold back the pain any longer, I double over and grab my head.

"Livia?" I hear the concern in Amah's voice.

"My head. The pain. It hurts."

I turn away and begin dry heaving, the nausea coming on strong. Why does my body feel as if it has been stomped on? Amah comes to my side. She takes my arm and helps me up. I keep my eyes shut tight.

"Make way! Let's get her in the wagon. You! Fetch some water."

Someone takes my other arm. "Can't she heal herself?" It's Reddik.

"I don't know." Amah replies. "There's so much we don't know about her gift."

Unable to see or move, I rely on Amah and Reddik's help with every step. They hoist me into the back of the wagon. A cup is brought to my lips. "En Oli, drink this."

The water is cold and refreshing. But it only gives my stomach something to reject. Tears fall down my face. "Amah, what's wrong with me?"

A soft blanket covers me and the touch of Amah's hand is cool against my forehead. "Shh. Relax. Try to guide your gift inside yourself."

The floor beneath me wobbles, and I hear the sound of creaking wheels starting into motion. I try to focus, but nothing happens. I place my hands on my head and try again.

Silence consumes me. The blackness that usually fills the background is now illuminated in gold. Reaching towards it, my body gets warmer. The closer I get, the warmer I become. Soon the warmth is too much but I can't step back. I hold my breath as a furnace overpowers me. The pain is numbing. When I force air out from my lungs, the hotness dissipates and a violet mist shrouds me, soaking into my skin.

I open my eyes, and the pain is gone. Darkness surrounds me as I wait for my eyes to adjust. The few minutes I thought it had taken to heal myself must've been hours.

I crawl to the edge of the wagon to the open flap. Small fires litter the darkness, illuminating guards standing watch. Their voices are kept low and I can't make out their conversations.

Amah and Reddik stand a distance away. Amah's arms are crossed, and Reddik shakes his head before walking away. I sigh. The people of Pynth are not ready for Amah's stubbornness.

I crawl under the blankets and snuggle against their warming comfort. Soon enough, sleep finds me.

I'M JARRED out of sleep. Blinking against the morning light, I realize we're on the move. I stretch out my arms and yawn. The pain and soreness from yesterday are gone.

I push my warm blanket away. The air is cold. Moving carefully, I reach for my cloak. When it's snug around my body, I push back a flap of canvas.

The Violet Guard ride close behind. They bow their heads to me. Butterflies sweep through me as I duck back inside. Once again the weight of expectation sinks back onto my shoulders.

The wagon stops and I stumble. Amah sticks her head inside.

"How do you feel?"

"Fine."

"Hmmph. So you were able to heal yourself after all?"

"It's hard to explain, but yes. Where are we?"

"We are two days from Pynth. If you come out and ride a bit, I can fill you in." My stomach growls in response. "And your belly."

I walk around the wagon and see Rosie. My heart leaps, and I rush to her, stroking her nose. She gently bumps me and I nuzzle against her.

Amah waits until I mount before handing me dried meat. As I eat the first strip, our company starts moving. Reddik is up front, leading.

"How did the Violet Guard get here so fast?"

"Oh, they aren't here for us." Amah replies. "They are here for Reddik and his brother. They came to bring them home. Tomorrow our guard should arrive. Which is fine. More protection for you."

THE REST of the day is uneventful. I spend most of my time either riding Rosie, or inside the wagon. Reddik checks on us from time to time, but keeps his distance for the most part.

When evening comes, Amah keeps me inside. She tells me it isn't proper to sit amongst the guard. Something seems off and it seems like she doesn't want me talking to anyone.

The next morning I'm once again riding alongside Amah —alone.

"I find it strange that no one talks to me. Are they afraid of me?"

"Don't be silly. They probably want to give you some space."

"Space? I've had that my whole life! I would think Regent

Grif's right-hand man would be more welcoming. Especially since I healed his brother, who also isn't talking to me. It's just strange."

Amah shifts uncomfortably. I know she's said something to them. I'm only waiting for her to confess. But she doesn't. And I'm not surprised.

On all those visits to Kale, no one spoke to me either—besides Annie. It was in those moments I used to pretend I had the Southern Kingdom's power of invisibility. I sigh. I no longer want to be invisible.

THE SNOW-COVERED surfaces fade out the closer we get to Pynth; winter is moving slower than our company, but soon it will catch up.

More of the Violet Guard arrive halfway through the day. It looks as if I will be having my own welcoming procession into Pynth. Inattentively, I watch Reddik up ahead issuing orders, and wonder how he became the Regent's right-hand man at such a young age. Will he be assigned to me when I become queen?

He turns and catches me staring. He smiles and waves. Ignoring the rushing warmth to my face, I wave back. By the blessing of Maker Adon, he *is* handsome.

He leaves the front and trots towards us.

"Your Royal Highness, Pynth is just over the horizon. Would you care to join me in front to have your first view of your beautiful city?"

Without looking to Amah for permission, I reply, "I would love to."

"Livia, I'm not.." Amah begins.

"Amah, please?"

Her lips purse before gently nodding for me to go on ahead.

I follow Reddik to the front of our procession. We pass by

Oliver, and he and I wave to one another. It's good to see him well.

"I want to thank you for healing him. It shames me to know I haven't said it before now," Reddik confesses.

"Oh! I am just glad we made it to him in time."

Reddik's mouth curves up. "Well, we both owe you a great debt. If there's anything you need, just ask."

"Thank you."

"Will the celebrations still be going on?" Amah asks from behind us.

"We should be arriving on the last day of the festivities," he replies. "It will be a gift to everyone, once they see who we are bringing through our gates. They'll not be expecting it."

"I can't wait to see it all," I exclaim.

"Well, wait no longer, princess. Behold the city of Pynth."

We ride over a small rise, and a grand wall stretches out to the horizon. The tops of buildings barely poke above it, teasing at what may be inside. In the distance, I see something that I've waited my entire life to view—Willobourne Castle.

Even from here I can see the intricate spires stretching high into the sky. I'm awestruck, and nearly urge Rosie to a gallop to get closer.

"Welcome home, Your Highness."

We proceed toward the main gate, across a field of grass. The scenery is magical and everything I imagined it would be. Harvested fields cover an area west of the fortified walls. The people working them are small dots to us.

"Is it everything you thought it would be?" Amah asks.

"Oh, Amah, it's all that and more. I can't believe I'm finally here." I bite my bottom lip. "What if they don't like me?"

Reddik laughs. "Princess, they've been waiting a long time for this moment. They'll adore you."

His comment catches me off guard but the look in his eyes seems honest, and I try to hide my admiration.

The city gate is massive, held together with great iron bands and nails. The hinges moan under its weight as it opens outward. I look up as we pass by, and the guards in the towers peer down. They are as curious of me as I am of them.

As we enter, the road widens into a large courtyard. Reddik leads us through it to a main road where shops with big windows and painted shutters line both sides, along with a street full of people gathered to see me.

The moment I appear, a thunderous cheer ripples through the air. They move to the sides of the road to let us pass by, but keep close enough to satisfy their curiosity. Their cheers fill my ears, and I can't help but smile when they call my name.

I admire the colorful clothes they wear—even the men. Like their clothes, their energy is full and bright. They wave excitedly, with unrestrained joy. Do I really mean this much to them?

The buildings behind them are grand; even the inns look elegant. There are so many different kinds of wares in the storefronts, from fine clothing made by seamstresses to items of steel from guild masters. The air tastes heavenly, and I see merchants standing out with trays of fresh baked goods. The smells beckons me in, and remind me how hungry I am.

White petals fall from the sky, distracting me from my want of food. Women with small children standing on balconies are releasing white petals from woven baskets. They swirl around gracefully, and the children down below try to catch them, collecting them in their pockets.

The joyous sound buzzing all around me is infectious and it gives me a confidence that I never knew I had. I look to Amah, but I find her gaze searching the crowd and being ever so watchful for any kind of threat. Even a city behind a well-guarded wall isn't enough to keep her at ease. I find Reddik

doing the same. I seem to be the only one enjoying this celebration.

We near a massive bridge made of white stone. At its
opposite end, towering high up into the sky, is Willobourne
Castle, a breathtaking sight. As we begin to cross over the
bridge, we see men lighting lamps hung on poles, preparing
for the oncoming darkness.

Birds squawk overhead and my eyes follow them as they
fly over a large stretch of deep blue water. Below the bridge,
soft waves cover the water's surface, bumping into large
boats that are coming back to shore. The sailors on deck see
me and wave from their vessels. I wave back.

I gaze over the enormous silhouette of the white stone
castle that's built on a mountain island of its own. I see
patches of trees on all levels, and windows are aglow, filled
with a soft yellow light.

We go through a huge gate that comes out from a thick
outer wall. The horses' hooves echo inside the long, arched
opening. My excitement turns to nervousness. Soon I will be
meeting Regent Grif—my uncle.

We come to the stables to where I can finally dismount.
Boys dressed in neat livery, with a white willow on their
vests, take Rosie over to a small field within the grounds.

"Are you ready to meet your uncle, My Lady?" Reddik
asks.

My stomach knots up and my hands become clammy.

"Yes, of course."

Amah takes me by the arm, and we both follow Reddik
across the courtyard and up the steps to the main doors. They
open into a vast chamber with vaulted domed ceilings.

Standing in the center of the large empty room is a tall
man with large muscles beneath a freshly pressed grey
uniform. His white hair is tied back at the nape of his neck,
and he looks intimidating with all the decorating pins and
medals spread across his chest. Next to him is the prettiest

woman I've ever seen, with the longest of red hair. She is dressed in a flowing blue gown. This has to be the Regent and his wife.

Reddik walks up to the Regent and converses quickly before he leaves the room. The Regent develops a scowl, but quickly smooths it away. He takes a step towards me, looking nervous himself.

"Welcome home, Princess Livia. I am Regent Grif, your uncle, and this is your aunt, Lady Ella." He turns and presents his wife, who bows her head slightly, her lips barely curving up. I can't tell if she is smiling or grimacing.

I swallow down my nerves. This formal meeting seems awkward, as my uncle and I both stare at one another, neither of us knowing what to do. Do I run over, and give him a hug?

Before I can give it much thought, he takes the remaining five steps between us and instinctively I rush to him and we embrace heartedly. So long I've wished for a family, and here it is before me.

He pulls back to get a closer look at me. I notice how much his features resemble my own, especially his straight narrow nose. His misty dark eyes mirror my emotions, and I brush away a tear that has escaped down my face.

"You look just like your mother," he says.

A smile spreads across my face. "Do I? I've never seen an image of her. I always hoped I would."

"Would you like to see one now?"

Not able to contain my excitement, I bounce up slightly. "Yes, please."

Regent Grif escorts me up a grand staircase that has a thin grey carpet going up its center. Lady Ella politely dismisses herself, letting me know it was nice to meet me. Her words, however, don't match her expression, leaving me feeling as if I've done something wrong.

"I'm glad you're finally here," my uncle says, interrupting my thoughts. "There's much for you to discover and learn about your kingdom. I hope you find that I've done my best to rebuild it, and to retain the memories of your parents' reign."

"I'm sure you've done brilliantly, Regent Grif. Much more than I'll ever do. My skills rest in nature, and I'm a bit overwhelmed by this whole new experience. I hope I'll catch on quickly and do what's needed of me."

What I really mean is, please don't leave me. I have no clue and I will fail. But I know I can't speak these thoughts. One thing I've learned from Amah all these years, is when you speak your doubt, it creates a seed that can grow into failure. I have always been told to refrain from making a bed that I could not get up from.

We continue through long corridors, ascending stairs that spiral around to the next level, to his study. Regent Grif pushes it open, revealing a dark room. He enters in first, and brings to life lamps set all around.

The room is spacious, able to fit a very large oak desk in its center. A fireplace is against the far wall, with two light-colored sofas to either side. My heart begins to pound when I see a rather large painting hung above the mantel. A powerful looking man is standing in magnificent violet robes, and a beautiful woman is positioned in front of him, sitting with her hands placed neatly in her lap. Her smooth white skin glows, along with her gorgeous white hair. I know instantly who they are—my parents.

My lips part, admiring the art that perfectly depicts them as I've always imagined them to look.

"The shape of your eyes and mouth are identical to your mother's. You even have the family nose." The Regent comes up next to me and points to my father. "Of course, that black hair of yours is from your father's bloodline."

I can see myself in both of them. From the raven black hair of my fathers, to the delicate features of my mother. I can't be any happier knowing how much alike we all look.

"I wish you had known them, En Oli." Amah approaches me, and stands at my side. My eyes shift down, and became glazed with a glassy layer of tears. "Me, too."

The Regent clears his throat. "Livia, I know you've only just arrived, but there are some things that were brought to my attention upon your arrival."

Amah steps forward, and my uncle's scowl returns.

"Yes, Amah. I'm aware of your secrets, and I would like to inform you of your ill judgment in keeping such things to yourself. I am surprised she hasn't been told already."

"She isn't ready," Amah says forcibly.

I look back and forth between the two. The tension in the air puzzles me.

"Are you really going to do this right now?" she says. "She's only just arrived, let her enjoy it."

"This is not my fault," he responds gruffly. "You should've told her a long time ago. Now you give me no choice."

Amah steps aside, defeated. She keeps her eyes downcast, avoiding my gaze. Worry gnaws at me. My uncle's eyes shut for a moment, and he takes a deep breath. I can't take the intensity anymore.

"Just tell me."

He opens his eyes, and I see regret reflected on his creased forehead. "You know the story of your parents and the raid from the East?"

"I do."

"What you don't know is they came for the newborn *heirs*. Amah was lucky enough to save you. However, she was unable to save the other. One Silent Watcher got away, and was able to smuggle your sister to the Eastern Kingdom."

"My sister? But I don't have a sister."

My eyes shift over to Amah, who refuses to look at me.

"Amah, what's he talking about?"

She looks up, tears shimmering in her eyes.

"It's true, En Oli. You have a sister, and she's your twin. I've kept it from you, and I'm sorry."

My stomach churns, and it feels like my heart just fell off the side of a cliff. Amah reaches out to me, but I recoil. "Don't."

I can't even look at her. Feeling this way is foreign, and all I want to do is run. This whole time that I've been hidden safely away, I've had a sister living with the malicious Eastern King?

Just moments ago, I was full of excitement and in awe. Now I'm plunged into another kind of reality and I'm unsure how to swallow it. My uncle's face is full of concern.

"I need a moment alone," I confess. "If you could take me to my room, please."

I refuse to break down in front of them. I need space and I need it now. My foundations have been shaken, and my world has turned over. I feel sick, and I don't want anyone to witness my breakdown.

11

GOLDEN MIRROR

THE MOMENT her eyes close to sleep, Livia enters back into the magical realm with the golden mirror. She stands before it once again. Her white gown flutters in a windless breeze. She peers into the mirror, but her reflection isn't there. She'd hoped to see the girl who looks like her, as she did before.

Having recently discovered she has a twin, she wonders if the girl in the mirror might be her sister. She plans on asking her, but a part of her is curious how the girl will respond. After all, if the girl is her sister, she's been living in the East for most of her sixteen years. Does she even know about Livia?

Livia steps closer to the mirror, and sees nothing.

Where is she?

Vera stays away from the mirror. The last time she peered into it, there was a girl standing there who looked like her, but wasn't her. She is almost afraid of what she will see if she stands before the mirror again. She wonders who that girl is, and what kind of magic the mirror holds. But she doesn't dare look. It could very well be the Enchanter.

In their dreams, both girls keep their eyes on the golden

mirror. One's curiosity is peaked, while the other remains wary. Their thoughts are of each other, and each promises herself that next time, questions will be asked.

12

VERA

THE LIGHT from the lantern helps guide me down into the forgotten chamber. I was allowed to leave my party over an hour ago and I'm now on my way to meet my friends. After the show I put on, the king insisted I stay awhile, ignoring the fact that I'd just killed a man known by many who were there.

Any opportunity the king has to expose my distress, he takes every time. I remember seeing Bellek's distaste. But what did he expect me to do in that situation? My hands were tied.

Reaching the damp corridor, I enter into a side chamber and set the lantern down on a broken table. No matter how hard I try to make this dank room into anything, it is useless. There are far too many cracks that let in moisture and there is nothing to hide the strong smell of mildew.

Finding a salvageable chair, I carefully sit and wait. My thoughts go to Zyrik. The king had him taken away after the killing. I hope he doesn't understand what I did, but the thought of him seeing me create chaos churns my stomach.

Tonight was just a taste of the control the king has over me. I worry what he'll have me do next. The last thing I want is to become a monster. Which is why I want to meet with my friends—I need advice.

My ears perk to the sounds of their voices. Nate, Karl, and Murrow push through the door mid conversation. Their voices fade when they see me.

Murrow whistles. "Hell, Vera, you didn't have to dress so nice just for us."

His smile melts away when he sees my stone face.

"What is it?" Nate says.

"The king had me use my gift to kill someone tonight." Their expressions darken. "Once again he used Zyrik to force me to do his bidding. I'm worried what other things he will have me do, now that my gift has manifested."

Murrow looks to the others, then to me. "What *is* your gift?"

"Didn't you hear what happened to Slyk?"

"Someone said one of your knives went through his eye, and his arm was broken. No one knows exactly how it happened. Kah announced how you deserved all ten lashes though—asshole."

"Oh. Would you like me to show you how I did it?" I wiggle my fingers at them.

Karl shakes his head. "How about you just tell us first. You did just say you killed someone."

I roll my eyes.

"Use it on me," Nate volunteers.

Murrow and Karl shake their heads and mutter "crazy" under their breath. I know Nate trusts me and I'm not surprised he'd be the one to step up to be tested.

I try to bring forth my gift, but nothing happens. I try again. Nothing.

Murrow looks over to Nate, and grins. "Looks like she has the gift of concentration."

My annoyance flares, and my gift surfaces. Nate turns and slaps Murrow across the face.

"Hey!" Murrow shouts.

I close off Nate's throat, and he frantically grabs at his neck. Karl and Murrow's eyes dart between us, and I can see they are full of confusion. When Nate begins to turn red, I release him.

He hunches over and coughs, trying to regain air back into his lungs. "Shit, Vera. What the hell did you just do to me?"

"I can control you."

"That was what you did to him?" Murrow gulps.

"Can you imagine all that I'm capable of now?"

Understanding passes over their faces.

"What are you going to do?" Karl asks, as he runs a hand over his mouth.

"She'll do what she's told, Karl. What other choice does she have?" Nate snaps. I sense his frustration; he always grasps things quicker than the others.

"Nate is right, I have no other choice. I fear the king has a plan for me, and it scares me to think what it could be. But I'm more scared for Zyrik. What if the king keeps his son at his side even more, just to make a point of how powerless I truly am?"

"You have to make the king believe his demands are what you want, too," Nate says. "If he sees you cooperate willingly, then he won't need to use Zyrik. The question is, can you do it?"

I chew over his suggestion, trying to analyze its practicality. What he says makes sense, but it means I'll have to think dark thoughts, and become someone I'm not. But for Zyrik's sake? I have no choice.

MORNING COMES, as does a message from the king requesting my attendance on him. I still have the image of the golden mirror and the strange girl from my dreams in my thoughts. The only thing that makes any sense to me is to believe the magic is showing me another side of myself. I wish there were someone I could ask. Maybe Bellek would know.

I tighten my leather bodice over my threads and look at my reflection. The tough outer shell I constantly display will be what I'll rely on to convince the king that I am his. Just as Nate said, if I can go along with the king's plans, Zyrik will be safe. I take a deep breath. I'll let that be my comfort.

I go to Zyrik's room and find him playing in the corner. A puppet is on each of his hands. I admire his innocence as he makes them dance in the air. How can a tortured boy like him bounce back from the nightmare of last night?

He turns and sees me, and promptly drops his puppets. He runs straight into my legs and holds on tightly.

"Oh, my! When did you get so strong?"

Zyrik shrugs his shoulders. I gently pull him free and pick him up, resting his head against my shoulder. He snuggles against my neck, and I laugh.

"Are you trying to tickle me?"

He giggles.

"Well, I think it's you that should be tickled."

I place him down and he runs shrieking. I chase him around for a while, then play with him and his puppets. I don't mention anything of last night and he doesn't seem to mind forgetting. When it is time for me to leave, he holds on even tighter. Leaving him is difficult and it takes me a few minutes to convince him of my return. Then I have to convince myself.

WALKING INTO THE WAR ROOM, I see a massive oak table taking up its center. The king is not yet here and the other chairs around the table are mostly occupied. I recognize only some of the men.

Captain Ryker sits at one end. His arms are crossed and a

smirk is plastered across his face. Does he know what the meeting's about? By his relaxed state, I would say he does.

Captain Leech sits at the opposite end. His expression is grim. He manages to give me a small smile as I go to sit by him.

There are other officials around the table, but I don't know them. They sit quietly, staring down at their laps, avoiding eye contact with everyone else at the table. I look around and take note of Bellek's absence.

A side door opens, and in walks the king, followed closely by Bruce and the Scree. Everyone stands until King Kgar motions for us to sit. Bruce remains standing, his eyes devoid of emotion.

King Kgar sits back and steeples his forefinger and thumb together as he looks to each of us. His gaze pauses upon me, and I notice the side of his mouth twitch. He snaps his fingers. "Map!"

One of the unknown officers flips out a map, and unrolls it. It extends the entire length of the table. I straighten in my chair and gaze at a detailed map of all four kingdoms. Every town, road, and river is marked clearly. Even The Wall is shown in perfect detail.

Another officer begins placing red and white tokens on different areas of the map, while the king patiently waits. Biting the inside of my cheek, my eyes roam over the others at the table. Leech is still wearing his grim expression, but Ryker is leaning forward eagerly.

When the two officers are finished, they promptly leave the room.

"Silent Watchers are trained for one purpose: to prepare for war," the king begins. "It's time we begin our quest for ultimate domination. The rules have now changed. We no longer need to rely on numbers." He glances over to me. "Not when a single thought can get the job done." My brow furrows. "I am promoting Vera to Commander."

My insides freeze. What did he just say?

Ryker clears his throat. "Your Majesty, if I may?"

"Oh, you may Ryker, but you will not change my mind. I have sent Bellek on a mission and Vera will be the Commander of my assassins. I don't believe there is anyone who can stop her."

Ryker sits back, seething with anger.

"I appreciate the honor, Your Majesty. I look forward to leading your men to victory," I reply.

"You have until the end of the week to prepare."

Leech and Ryker jump up. "That's impossible, Your Majesty!"

Kgar ignores their protest. His eyes lock on mine, waiting for me to challenge him. But I'm to take Nate's suggestion. Whatever the king wants, he gets. All for Zyrik.

"As you wish, sir."

The captains share an incredulous look.

"Great! I am glad someone here understands my agenda." Kgar rests his hands on the table. "Now, what is your plan?"

I panic. "Plan?"

"To get my assassins to Pynth."

I rack my brain and try to recall all the times I have over-heard Bellek.

"We will go through the northern section of The Wall. It's guarded least well."

"What makes you think that?" Ryker interrupts. "It would be better to just storm through the main gate. They won't be expecting us to storm it."

"If we use the main gate, we won't have the element of surprise," I reply cooly. "And isn't that what we pride ourselves on, Captain?" Ryker's lips purse. "Anyway, as I was saying, I'll take their minds, and then we'll tear down a section of The Wall. We get through, then we journey under cover of the pines. It will be something they won't expect— thousands of assassins suddenly on their doorstep.

"Captains, dismissed!" The king barks.

Ryker leaves with a scowl, but Leech grins, and pauses before leaving. "Commander, I've been working on a project. I believe it will help us in the war."

"I will meet with you this afternoon. Thanks, Captain," I answer.

Leech nods firmly, and exits the room.

"I must say, Vera, I'm surprised by your change of attitude. Your willingness is exactly what I need. This promotion of yours will test your loyalty to me. Soon you will have to make a decision. Don't disappoint me."

I know better than to ask. "Yes, sir."

"However, you have already disappointed me in another matter." He claps twice. The doors open back up and two Silent Watchers drag in a beaten assassin; his head is covered. "I make rules, and I expect those rules to be followed. If not, punishment will be enforced. Do you understand what I'm saying?"

"Yes, sir."

"I don't think you do." He walks around the table. "You see, Vera, while I am a tolerant king I expect obedience. For example, when I order that no one is to touch something that is mine, I expect that rule to be followed."

My muscles tense. Kgar rips off the cover off the assassin's head. Pain bursts through my chest, lungs, and throat. I don't even recognize Marcus. Both his eyes are swollen shut.

"Well, do you have anything to say?"

I can't breathe.

"Come. I want you to witness what happens to those who touch what is mine." I stand as he signals Bruce over.

The two Silent Watchers force Marcus's head down while Bruce unsheathes his sword. My heart beats fast. Bellek warned me about playing with fire. Now, I am to be burned.

Bruce raises his sword and it comes down swiftly.

"No!" I scream.

His arm freezes, the blade stops against Marcus's neck.

King Kgar snarls and smacks me across my face. "You dare use your gift against my command?"

The Scree hurries to the king's side. She whispers words I can't hear. After a few long minutes, King Kgar shouts, "Enough!" Without looking at me he leaves the room. I force Bruce to follow, worried he might attempt to finish the job on Marcus.

"Take him to my chambers," the Scree demands. Marcus turns his head in my direction. His face might be unrecognizable but there is no denying how grateful he looks for being alive. The guards drag him away.

"What will become of him?" I blurt out.

"Whatever I want." The side of her mouth curls up. "He's mine now." She turns and leaves.

I breathe a sigh of relief. At least he's still alive.

THREATENING grey clouds overhead give off the scent of rain. The horse beneath me doesn't seem to mind. Provena is one of the largest stallions in stock. His training has taken him through every brutal scenario, including harsh weather conditions. Provena is sturdy, taking the uneven terrain sure-footedly as I lead him behind the Silent Tomb.

The Silent Tomb has been around since the beginning. It was built to house dead warriors. When a Silent Watcher dies, his body is burned in a ceremony. His ashes are then collected, and placed inside the tomb.

It's an honor to be buried here. And those Watchers denied the honor are forever disgraced in the afterlife. Their souls are trapped in our world, wandering aimlessly—never resting.

Off in the distance, thunder rolls. It interests me why Captain Leech wants to meet me here. Men are tying down heavy canvases over what seem to be very large cages. A screeching sound pierces from one of them.

Captain Leech comes out of a tent and jogs to my side. "Commander Vera!"

I frown. "Captain."

"I just got them covered and ready to go."

"Keppers? You've been collecting Keppers?"

"Training, I've been training Keppers," he grins widely.

I shake my head. I thought Leech was a normal, level-headed captain. Now I see that can't be further from the truth.

"How in the world did you manage to train these beasts?"

"Patience," he answers.

Not only can Keppers rip you to shreds, they are the only beasts in the vast mountain range that managed to survive the loss of magic. These birds are the size of Bruce, their talons unforgiving. They rip apart anything that comes their way. If Leech really did train these birds, they will wreak havoc on the enemy.

I can't help but smile. Captain Leech has shown me the impossible is possible. Our enemies will never see this coming.

"How many?" I ask.

"I have five that are fully trained, and another three that are not far behind."

"I expect you to have them all under control by the time we reach Pynth."

His jaw tightens. "Understood, Commander."

I RIDE over to Graves Hill to meet with the men. It's time they hear the news and begin to prepare. I reach the center of the arena, and signal for a banging on the drum.

I look to the murky clouds above me, and hope the rain stays away just a while longer; I need the men to hear me. I patiently wait until the arena is a black sea of assassins. Nate,

Karl, and Murrow stand off to the side, confusion etched on their faces.

The beat of the drum stops when Ryker and Leech join me up on the stage, putting the arena into complete silence.

"I'm to inform you of recent changes issued by King Kgar. Commander Bellek has been sent on a mission, and I am promoted in his place."

They look to one another, doubt clear on all their faces.

"I have trained with all of you. You never saw me as a girl, or a prisoner, but as a fellow fighter. Some of you even hate me, but still you treat me as one of your own. I've stood up to every single one of you, and even though I was kicked on my ass, your asses were kicked, too."

Men nod, their lips twitch with humor.

"I know this all might not make sense to you, but I promise I will do what I can to secure us a victory. You are the ones I want at my back, you are the ones I trust. I know that no matter what, you will fight until you can no longer."

I attempt to put much fierceness behind my words. I want them to know I mean what I say.

"I have a gift that will aid us. I'm able to reach inside minds and manipulate their bodies, forcing those bodies to do what I want them to. I plan to use this ability to help take down the enemy. I swear I will never use my gift on you without your knowledge, unless it's for self-defense, or to prevent your death. You are mine and I am yours!"

From those in front to all the men in the back, they throw their fists in the air and shout, "Watch!" The faces of my friends are full of pride.

The king has never understood that loyalty is earned, not bought or demanded. But Bellek understands, and so do I.

Rain finally breaks through the dark clouds and I end our meeting. Now we prepare.

. . .

I REACH Black Ridge Castle by nightfall, having helped organize what supplies are needed. I run up the stairs, a sense of excitement coursing through me. I'll finally be leaving this place—even if it's only for a time.

I notice a shadow following close behind. I pull my gift to the surface and turn quickly.

"Hey, Vera."

I suck air through my teeth. "Marcus!" His face is no longer swollen and the blood is gone. No healing herbs known to men could have healed him so quickly. This is the work of the Scree.

He moves close to me and lowers his voice. "Thanks for saving me."

My heart thumps hard inside my chest. It seems forever since I've been with him, and I'm thankful he is alive.

"I thought the Scree owned you now?"

His dark blue eyes have an intensity about them, and I feel a sudden ache inside my body.

"She doesn't own me; she only saved me from King Kgar's wrath. After she healed me, she said I could leave. So I did." His hand brushes my arm and my flesh tingles.

"Aren't you worried about being caught by the king again? The Scree won't be able to talk him out of killing you a second time."

"I heard you would be leaving soon. I just wanted to see you."

I realize now how lonely I've been feeling. I know this relationship can get him killed, but here he is, still wanting me. How can I deny him?

We hurry to my chamber. We can't chance being caught. Once my chamber door closes, we entangle one another. Marcus lifts up my chin exposing my neck. I hold my breath as his lips press against its base, then slowly work their way up to my face. A strong awareness of my own heartbeat echoes in my ears.

He lifts me up and I wrap my legs around him as he carries me to my bed. He lowers me carefully down, and begins to remove my leathers. My nerve endings tingle as they are exposed to the cool air.

After he takes his garments off he joins me. My lips part as he stares at me. I've never seen him so hungry for me before. Finally he takes me, and I tremble. We get lost in time as we enjoy each other's company. I know I have things to do, but my duties as Commander can wait.

13

LIVIA

A MASS of red-masked assassins surrounds me. Among them is a girl in full black armor with violet eyes, who has her blade pointed towards me.

I jerk awake.

Breathing heavily, I stare at the golden canopy that towers high above me. It was only a dream. I sigh with relief.

Morning light creeps out from behind thick cream-colored drapes to spread across the room—my parents' room to be exact. I was in a state of confused anger last night, and I was not prepared to be taken to my parents' chambers. Regent Grif might've seen this as a nice gesture, but it only added to the pain.

The moment he left, I cried. The life that was taken from me came out in the form of tears.

When I finally was able to doze off, I entered straight into the dream world with the golden mirror. I remember feeling determined to get answers. But the girl never showed herself. The girl—my sister.

A weight settles once again in my stomach, as Amah's betrayal is fresh on my mind. How could she so easily have kept my sister from me? Though she saved me and raised me as her own. The battle that rages inside delivers a sense, a feeling I've never experienced before. Everything feels wrong —unnatural.

I push the heavy quilt aside and slide off the biggest bed I have ever seen. The soft rugs that cover the floor cushion my feet as I cross over to the double doors that lead into the sitting room.

My heart pounds inside my chest as I see this space where my parents once lived. The ceiling of the huge room domes up, with wood beams running the entire length of the room. The walls are of smooth stone, and are covered with richly colored tapestries. There is also a fireplace, with white columns to its side. Comfortable sofas and chairs covered with rich fabric are placed about the room, with some arranged neatly in front of the fireplace. I can imagine my parents sitting there together after a long day. This is where they would have had their quiet moments.

Across the room, double doors, with small panes of glass, are covered over with sheer, lavender curtains. As it was late the previous night and I was overcome with exhaustion, I haven't yet viewed what lies beyond.

Crossing the room, I open the doors, revealing an expansive balcony overlooking the city of Pynth. I shouldn't be surprised the king and queen should have had the best view in the kingdom, but this is incredible.

I breathe in the clean fresh air of morning, and let it out slowly through my nose. Now it's time to face the day.

I go and wash my face before sorting through a wardrobe my uncle pointed out the night before. It's packed full of colorful fabrics, and they appear to be all dresses—something I've never worn.

I pull out a frilly green dress with multiple layers. My upper lip curls in distaste. I put the dress back, and skim through the others. Amah and I never had a reason to wear dresses. We spent our time hunting, or climbing trees. Dressing for fine dining was never in our daily schedules.

I finally come across a grey dress that looks to be somewhat tolerable. I put it on and it immediately feels foreign. It sits off my shoulders, and the sleeves hug my arms all the way to my wrists. There the sleeves flare out and split past my wrists into white lace.

I view myself in the mirror and I'm pleasantly surprised. This dullest color in the wardrobe matches my eyes perfectly. I use a brush to untangle my hair, and the long dark layers hang beautifully down my shoulders. I barely recognize myself.

A knock comes at my door. Taking one last look at myself, I go to answer it. Regent Grif stands there, looking sharp.

"Ah, Princess Livia. I'm pleased to see you awake. Would you care to join me for breakfast?"

"I would love to, Regent Grif." He extends his arm and I take it.

"You can call me Grif, or Uncle. No need for formality among family."

"Yes, Re—I mean, Uncle."

The corner of his mouth quirks up. "I hope you slept well?"

"I did—eventually." My smile fades.

"I'm sorry your first night came with such heavy news. It's not how I wanted your first moments to be."

I have no desire to discuss Amah right now, so I change the subject. "Will we be joining Lady Ella?"

"Yes, of course. And my two children."

"Oh! You have children?"

"Yes, two. Though Hal is no longer a child, but a young man now. He's a captain in the Violet Guard. My youngest is five. Her name is Kimber and she believes she's the one in charge."

I attempt to smile. These children are another revelation.

The more I uncover the truths about my life, the more I doubt who I really am. But I can't let Amah's mistakes keep me down. There's so much more to discover and appreciate. "They both sound wonderful. I can't wait to meet them."

He squeezes my arm as we continue down the hall. I glimpse more of Willobourne through the large windows. The castle is vast, with courtyards below, and balconies along the neighboring towers. It's a forest of its own and I can't wait to explore it.

My brief joy melts away as I think of Amah not being at my side. A sadness creeps over me. I can't continue feeling this way; I have to talk to her.

A movement behind a large flower pot catches my eye. I glimpse a small child with a headful of bright red curls.

Grif whispers out from the corner of his mouth. "Pretend you don't see her."

Startled by his request, I barely manage to keep my poise as I avoid looking at her.

When we pass the child, we hear a soft giggle. My uncle squeezes my arm and keeps our pace casual. After a few moments, he releases my arm and quickly jumps around into a crouch. "Aargh!"

The child playfully screams, jumps back and then into his arms.

"Papa!"

Regent Grif laughs and nuzzles this little girl who can only be his daughter. He gently places her down and the bright-eyed child turns to me. Her eyes grow wide. "Oh, Papa. Her eyes are so pretty. Can I have violet eyes, too?"

The innocent question makes us laugh.

"I'm afraid not, little one." Her smile fades, and she pouts out her bottom lip. "Kimber, this is your cousin, Princess Livia."

Kimber's pout quickly turns upward, and she gives me her best curtsy. "Welcome home, princess."

"Thank you, Lady Kimber."

"You are the prettiest person I have ever seen," she confesses.

"Oh, why thank you!"

I admire the perfect red curls that frame her porcelain face. I remember passing by a storefront in Kale that displayed a doll that looked just like her. If anything, *she* is the prettiest person I've ever seen.

"Okay, Kimber, run off and find your mother. Tell her we're on our way."

"Yes, Papa." She turns and begins skipping down the hall.

Grif links his arm back with mine.

"She is adorable!" I exclaim.

His mouth quirks up. "She's my joy."

THE WHOLE TOWN of Kale could easily fit inside the walls of the Great Hall. Windows line the sides of one wall with a large bay window in its center. The opposite wall holds a massive stone fireplace, with the mounted heads of game animals above its mantel.

Ready servants line the room in matching pressed lavender blouses and dark grey leggings. We pass between four long wooden tables to the front, where the high table is placed. Silverware and plates are set out, with flowers and greenery displayed for fresh decor.

My aunt enters wearing a gown that resembles the frilly dress I discovered earlier—only hers is in layers of cream. Kimber is holding her hand, and her face stretched into a wide grin.

"Isn't she beautiful, mother? Me and cousin Livia are going to be great friends!"

Lady Ella scowls. Kimber slumps her shoulders. Her mother whispers something sharp and Kimber straightens back up. She gives me an unconvincing smile.

My aunt meets my gaze, and her smile seems stale. I don't understand why she is coming across so cold, but I find it unnerving.

Lady Ella motions for us to take our seats. The Regent sits at the table's center, with Lady Ella on his right and me on his left. Kimber sits next to me, her legs bouncing with excitement as she settles in her chair at my side.

The side door opens once again, and several servants enter, placing bowls of porridge in front of us. The scent of cinnamon wafts to my nose, and the aroma is amazing. I take my spoon and go to scoop up my first bite.

Lady Ella clears her throat. "I know you're not accustomed to the ways here at the castle, but it's customary to wait for the head of the table first."

I set my spoon down and place my hands in my lap; warmth fills my cheeks. The Regent smiles apologetically. He quickly picks his spoon up and begins to eat. Everyone follows suit, and I make sure I'm the last one to join in.

The double doors open, and in walks a young soldier; his blond hair is neatly slicked back.

"Princess Livia, I am Hal, your cousin," he bows.

"Nice to finally meet you, Captain Hal."

His face brightens. "Likewise, princess. It's been a long time coming. The men are glad to see that you are safely back home."

"Oh! Well, I appreciate their concern!"

"There is a council meeting later this morning," Regent Grif says to his son, "I would like you to attend."

"Yes, father."

Hal seats himself next to Kimber, and leans over to rub noses with her.

"Hal!" Lady Ella pins him with her sharp eyes.

Hal and Kimber laugh quietly as a bowl of porridge is placed in front of him. I bite the inside of my cheek to keep from smiling. Yes, this is indeed my family.

After breakfast my uncle escorts me to his study.

"I know you've just discovered you have a sister, but there are things that I believe need to be explained."

My heart migrates to my throat.

"When your sister was discovered missing, we thought her dead. In truth, we thought both of you dead."

"You keep saying my sister. Do you know her name?"

"Vera."

I breathe in deep. Vera.

"My father, in the North, knew the West needed to be rebuilt, so he sent me. Not long after I arrived, letters from Amah begin to arrive, and we confirmed you were alive. Vera was also confirmed alive shortly after. There were many times I felt here is where you needed to be. But I was advised against it," he frowns slightly. "Pynth wasn't safe."

I recall Amah's refusal. My uncle had had no choice.

"The thing is, Livia, that Vera has been raised by assassins. The same ones that hunt you. Who knows where her loyalties lie. Like you, I'm afraid, she doesn't know the entire story. But the Western Kingdom will soon be yours. It'll be up to you to decide how to handle her…umm, situation."

"How do you expect me to make the right decision? Doesn't she have a right to rule as well?"

"You were firstborn. The Crown will always be yours while you live, even should your sister find herself at your side." He leans forward. "I'll not abandon you. But I believe you will find inside yourself the strength of your parents. You will find greatness."

I wipe my hands on my dress. "I don't know if I should be sad, angry, excited, or scared. Right now, I feel all of them."

He smiles. "Your mother was terrified when she came to this kingdom. I came with her those many years ago, encouraging her and offering comfort. I promise, just like your mother, you will be fine."

I chew on my bottom lip. "Can you tell me more of her?"

His face softens as he leans back in his chair. "She was my beloved sister. The only daughter of five children—my father's pride and joy." He smiles painfully then huffs out a laugh. "Your father was so ever determined to have her at his side. I wish you could have known him, your father. He was charming and he always knew what to say. Just between you and me, he taught me the meaning of practical jokes."

"My father did?"

"Oh, yes. I remember when your father was trying to get my sister alone to ask for her hand in marriage. The problem was she had a very nasty handmaiden who never left her side. He had me assist him by putting blue ink in the flowers in your mother's garden. He hoped when the old maid stooped to smell the flowers, the ink would send her away from Kyra's side. Unfortunately, that's not how it played out. He chose my sister's most beloved flower. So it was your mother who found those freshly-inked petals. Before he could warn her, she had already taken her first whiff; blue ink went everywhere."

"And my mother still married him?"

"Yes!" he laughs. "I was sure in the moment she would hate him. But you know what your mother did when she discovered her face blue? She laughed. And then shoved the flower in your father's face, giving his face the same look."

I can't help but laugh. This is the type of story I've wanted to hear. "It seems they really loved each other."

"They adored one another. It was a match made by Maker Adon himself. In that moment, I knew he would take wonderful care of her."

The room becomes quiet. There is so much I don't know about my mother and father. I'm glad I now have an uncle to paint these wonderful stories. I don't care they also sadden me; the happiness I feel by hearing them overpowers it.

"There is a council meeting I must attend. If you care to,

you may join me. You won't be expected to speak, but you can get a glimpse into the happenings of your kingdom."

"I think that sounds okay."

"Livia, I know you've lived out in the pines your entire life, but the blood that flows through your veins is of royalty. You share the same blood as all the queens and kings before you. You'll find that you are capable of many things, and I have complete faith in you."

My spirits rise slightly, hearing him speak of my potential. I know next to nothing but I also know I can't let my parents down. I need to stop being scared and be determined to learn what I can. There's no turning back to the pines. Even if I could, I wouldn't belong. Here is my home. My true home.

"Do you mind if I speak with Amah first?"

"But of course. I understand how difficult this has been for you. Just know that in all my life the sooner I've known important information, the sooner I've been able to address the problem, and my enemies couldn't use it against me."

"It's okay, uncle. This is information I should've known a long time ago. It would've hurt no matter when I heard it." Which is the truth. "Will I have time to come for the council meeting?"

"I won't start without you. In fact, I plan to escort you there myself. And Amah can come, too, if you'd like her to."

"But won't you be late?"

A sparkle forms in his eyes. "They can't start without me."

The Regent takes me to Amah's room. It isn't far from my own. Of course he would place her next to me. She is, after all, my caretaker. He says he'll come back after a while, to give me and Amah plenty of time to talk out our issues. I thank him and he leaves. Now I'm standing at her door—staring at it.

I knock softly. A moment passes before the door opens. She wears a simple white blouse tucked in dark trousers, and a stone-faced expression.

"Can we talk?" I blurt out.

She nods. I'm about to take a step forward, when she steps out and closes the door behind her.

"How about we take a walk?" she says.

She leads me down a few levels onto a simple balcony. A breeze flows through the air and I smell the faint scent of salt from the sea below.

Amah turns and faces me, her expression full of regret and pain. "I am so sorry, En Oli."

I try to swallow down the lump in my throat.

"I don't know how to feel right now about you keeping this secret from me," I say. "What I do know is that I can't do what they expect of me without you. I don't hate you, but it will take time for me to trust you again. You have to be honest with me. I can't be kept in the dark about important matters that affect me."

"You are right to be upset with me."

"Amah…"

"I should have told you about your sister. It was my own selfishness that kept it from you. When your parents were killed and I knew she was taken, I had no idea what became of her. All I knew was that I had to escape with you and go into hiding. I knew they would come looking for you. Many times I thought you were old enough to know the truth. However, those many times I was also led to other thoughts: What will she do if she knows? Will she try to find her sister? Will she walk into danger, not knowing that the king is hunting her? No, I could not tell you."

Amah knew me well. I would've wanted to go after my twin, especially knowing what the Eastern King was capable of. But now I do need to find her, and bring her back. She's my other half and my family. A family I have so longed to have.

"Regent Grif said that no one has gone after her this whole time and now it's up to me, what to do."

Amah raises her head curiously. "He said that to you?"

"Yes."

"And what are your thoughts?"

It comes out in a whisper, but I say it all the same, "I want her here where she belongs."

"And I'll help you if it's the last thing I do. I might have hidden this information from you, but all these years I've tortured myself knowing Vera was somewhere out there. For so long, I've wanted to go get her, but I couldn't risk you. Now that you know, I'll be the first to help you on this mission. You are right, here is where she belongs."

We embrace fiercely.

"Do you think she has the healing gift as well?" I ask.

Amah looks out over the balcony. "It is the gift of the Western Kingdoms heirs, so it could be. If only there were a way to make sure."

I am about to mention the dream I've been having about the golden mirror, but I stop myself. I don't know why I feel the need to keep it a secret, but I feel this experience is my own, and I'm not ready to share it. So I leave Amah to ponder, and decide to make a point of trying to find the answer myself.

We enter the council chamber, and sit in two empty seats next to the Regent. I feel nervous being in a full room of strangers, and I keep my eyes focused on my feet.

"I call this meeting to order. First, I want to introduce Princess Livia to you."

Everyone gives me a warm welcome. I look up for just a moment, and see how thrilled they are to be in my presence. Some even wave to Amah.

Reddik is among them and he winks when we make eye contact. My skin flushes, and I look back down. I saw Hal sitting next to him a moment ago, but I don't dare look back their way again.

"Commander Barrett, if you will." My uncle continues.

A man with jet black hair and wearing a crisp grey uniform straightens in his chair. He has a broken nose, which shows a degree of experience others in the room don't have. For such a young man, his presence alone commands the room.

"I received word the East is planning to move against us—and soon." He clasps his hands in front him on the table. "I've already begun preparations. The outer wall is being strengthened, and weapons checked and sharpened. They will find themselves at a disadvantage when our preparations are finished, sir."

"I knew word of Livia's return would reach the king quickly enough," the Regent chimes in. "His insistence on having both of these girls is what makes him so predictable."

Soft mummers circle the table; all are alert except for an old man across from me whose chin rests on his chest, apparently sleeping.

The Regent follows my gaze.

"Scholar Eli."

The old man doesn't respond. Regent Grif raises his voice. "Scholar Eli!"

Eli jerks awake. "W-What did I miss?"

"Nothing of much importance. Just that the East is marching our way to capture our newly acquired princess."

Scholar Eli licks his lips. "Well, of course the East is in motion. Are you really surprised by this information?"

I can't help but suppress a smile. He is peculiar, and I take to liking him immediately. His cloudy eyes shift to mine, and I quickly avert my eyes back down to my lap.

"The question we should be asking ourselves is, how can we use our princess to gain theirs? They both have a gift, yes?" Eli asks.

This time muttering circles the room, but the Regent silences it. "We will not *use* Princess Livia. But, yes, the more we know of the gifts, the more we can rely on Princess Livia to help us defend ourselves."

Scholar Eli continues studying my face. "If I might ask the princess a question?"

I nod.

"Have you heard of Queen Bellflower?"

I sit forward, and wipe my palms on my dress.

"I have."

"Would you be interested to learn more about her and the magic she's bequeathed you?"

When I look at Amah, her eyes narrow. But just past her, an entertaining grin on Reddik's face catches my attention. It reminds me of my excitement as a child, yearning for magic. This is what I've been waiting for since the moment I discovered my gift—knowledge.

"I would love to know everything, Scholar Eli."

"Well, in that case, I know the exact place in which we can find everything to know."

When he sees my confused expression, he adds, "The Temple in Willow Round, of course."

Willow Round! Excitement rushes through my veins. I finally get to see the Willow!

14

VERA

THE WALL IS AN ENORMOUS STRUCTURE, made of rock taken from the mountains. It's built on the edge of Wolfmere Peaks and stretches down to the West's southern shores.

Years and years ago, when the East tried with their greater strength to conquer the West, the West united with the North to push them back. Then the West and North together wove magic into The Wall.

When magic died, the magic in The Wall died too. But The Wall is still a formidable barrier. There's only one entrance and the West guards it diligently.

This is why I have to march the Silent Watchers along Wolfmere Peak to the least guarded part of The Wall. With the help of my gift, I hope to secure this section.

Provena paws at the ground and blows impatiently. The week has flown by fast, and we're now standing at the edge of a batch of thinned pines, facing The Wall. Thousands of assassins stand behind me, awaiting my command.

A command that would have come from Bellek—if he were here. Instead he's out on an errand for the king. A message from him arrived earlier this morning.

It read along these lines: knowing that I was to be made

Commander, that there were those who would not be ready to accept it, and to watch my back. But I knew all that already. What I didn't know was in the second part of his message, about a friend of his. How he would be keeping an eye on me. It had irritated me at first, as if Bellek didn't trust me. But I brushed away the negative emotions. I have only few in my life I can trust. And he is one of them.

"Commander," Leech speaks, "we are ready."

I walk Provena out onto the open field. My eyes shift over to the mountains and I wonder if Bellek's friend is watching me now. Supposedly a coin engraved with the markings of a dove's head will be presented to me, a token of peace.

My focus returns to The Wall. Doubt creeps to the edges of my thoughts. Will my magic reach that high?

My red Commander cloak spreads out behind me—a late gift from the king. I can still feel his slimy hands over my body from his early morning visit. I hadn't expected him. It took seeing Zyrik afterwards to put my mind back on my task.

The Violet Guard gather with their bows drawn. Their bodies twitch, showing their hesitancy as they see a girl approach. I count fifty, but I know there are more.

I embrace the Western chill air. It's foreign, like the magic that thrills through my veins. But it's also comforting.

"Hold your position and state your business," a guard shouts over the edge.

It starts with a simple thought and my gift sparks.

Fifty guards step to the ledge, and throw themselves off The Wall. Their bodies thud hard against the solid ground with the sound of shattering bones.

Two heads barely pop over the ledge, and I grab hold of their minds and send them to their deaths as well. Arrows begin to soar over, the remaining guards shooting blindly toward an unseen target. I move closer to The Wall to avoid the random flights of arrows.

Watching for any movement, I wait patiently, keeping my mind quick. Twenty more guards look over the ledge to assess the damage, and soon enough my mind locks onto theirs, and I burst their hearts inside their chests.

Minutes drag on until I'm sure there are no guards left. A subtle pounding settles behind my eyes. Ignoring the pain, I place two fingers in my mouth, and whistle.

Catapults are pushed forward and set. Giant boulders are released to crash into The Wall. We have to make a large enough hole for the assassins to pass through easily.

Some time passes before The Wall begins to crumble. Violet Guards continue to appear, but before their arrows can find targets, they are dead.

Before long I am leading Provena through a gaping hole into a kingdom I thought I'd never see. Thousands of black pines stretch out before me, a dusting of snow brushing their tops. My lips part, then curve up. The snow is beautiful.

"Happy to be home?" My eyes snap to Captain Ryker's mocking grin.

"Must you always be an ass, Captain? Go find someone else to annoy. I have no need of your pointless observations."

Ryker's sneer disappears and I nudge my horse forward. He really is a prick. We travel west, maneuvering through the thick pines before Leech rides to my side.

"Commander."

"Captain Leech."

"What you did back there was impressive. The men think so as well. If there were any who doubted you, they no longer do."

Pain shoots through my head, and I clamp my eyes shut.

"Commander? Are you all right?"

"I'm fine. It's just a headache."

We finally stop to make camp, and I barely find my tent before passing out into darkness.

15

GOLDEN MIRROR

FIVE MORE STEPS FORWARD, and Vera will find herself standing directly in front of the golden mirror. The pain in her head is gone, and she wonders if the relief of pain is her dream's doing.

The strange girl is standing across from her, and Vera sees her lips moving. It's as if she is trying to tell her something, but nothing is coming out.

Vera: *Hello? Who are you?*

The girl speaks again, but once again Vera cannot hear her. This girl looks exactly like her but something is off. She knows she doesn't have any other family and thinks maybe the Enchanter is somehow linked to the mirror, trying to put thoughts inside her head. Vera was hoping this mirror would provide answers, but she finds it only confusing.

Livia is frustrated. She doesn't understand why her sister can't understand her. When she sees Vera attempt to speak, she can't hear her. Livia wonders how she is supposed to find out about her sister if they can't speak to one another. Livia knows the East will be coming, but she doesn't know if her sister knows about her, or knows that she might be hunting her sister unknowingly. Livia has to find out how to use this golden mirror. Before it is too late.

16

LIVIA

I ADMIRE myself in the mirror wearing a beautiful fur cloak. An attached note says it is from Lady Ella, that she hopes any trips outside the castle will find me warm.

Unsure what to make of the nice gesture, I can't help but smile at how the cream-colored fur makes me feel like royalty. Maybe my aunt likes me after all?

I wear a fitted blue dress underneath that wraps delicately around my shoulders. The cloak is welcome; with the dropping temperatures that befell us during the night, coldness would have settled quickly under the thin material of my dress.

"Lady Ella sent you this, this morning?" Amah asks.

"Yes. The note she left is lying over there on the table." I grab a silver belt and latch it around my waist.

After speaking with my uncle, we decided a trip to see Scholar Eli would be helpful. He and Amah both find him strange, but they know he is the best person for me to talk to about my gift.

He lives inside the Temple, and only travels out to attend council meetings. He lives and breathes the books inside the Temple.

I hold up another belt—it has a buckle the size of a dinner plate—I quickly place it back. I look back into the mirror, and see Amah in the mirror's reflection. She is gazing intently over the note, reading it as though it holds a cryptic message. She doesn't trust this Lady Ella; that's clear in the furrow of her brow.

When she catches me staring, her face softens.

"You look lovely, En Oli."

We go down to meet my uncle in the main hall. He embraces me the moment I arrive, and I breathe in his musky scent. Something tugs inside my chest; it reminds me of the woods I left behind.

"It amazes me how much you resemble both of your parents. The people will think they've come back to life," Regent Grif says.

He looks over my shoulder. I turn to find Reddik approaching. I try to ignore the flutter inside myself.

"Are you coming too?" I ask.

"Of course. I wouldn't miss your second outing amongst your people. Besides, someone has to look after the Regent. The Maker himself wouldn't leave that man alone."

The Regent laughs. "Now, Reddik. Just because *you* know the truth, doesn't mean you have to go telling everybody." He slides me an amused glance, and I stifle a laugh.

We head outside to the courtyard where our horses are waiting. A young stable boy with a tangled mess of curly black hair stands next to Rosie.

"Oliver!" I wave excitedly to him, and hurry to his side. "How good it is to see you."

"It's good to see you too, Your Royal Highness." A smile spreads across his face as he puffs out his chest. I notice the willow emblem on his livery, and I can tell he is proud to wear it.

"Are you doing well?" I ask.

"Oh yes, princess. My brother was able to work out a deal with the stable master to make sure I handle your horse. I must say, Rosie is good natured and makes my work easy."

"Oh, really? Just be careful if you come around her with any sweets that you don't plan to share; you'll find another side of her that's not so pleasant."

He snorts a laugh.

Reddik and the others come over to say hello, then mount their steeds. I lean forward and whisper in Oliver's ear. "Are you truly doing okay?"

He puffs out his cheeks. "I'm still sad, but it's getting better."

I place my hand on his shoulder, and he tenses. "Don't hesitate to ask for anything you need."

Oliver's shoulders relax. "Thanks, my Lady."

He takes my hand and assists me up to my saddle. I take the reins and guide Rosie over to the others, where I see Reddik staring at me with a peculiar expression. I can tell he wants to ask me something, but he doesn't. Instead he smiles and leads our party out onto the bridge.

Crossing over the bridge seems different this time around. Now there's a soft sky above, and the lacy waves below rock gently against the shore. Birds fly overhead, masters of the salty updrafts, and I find them captivating.

This scenery is the complete opposite of what I am used to. It seems fresh and busy. When we pass by the people of Pynth, their eyes shine as they wave, embracing me with their warm welcomes. As we get further inside the city, I find the love of the people expressed in ways I never knew existed. They stand around and listen to our hooves of our horses clattering against the cobblestone streets as we pass them by, shouting their welcomes and compliments.

Reddik brings his horse up next to mine.

"I told you they would adore you."

"Yes, you did." My head whips around when I hear my name called out behind me, and I wave back in response. "How did you know they would?"

"You must understand, princess. It's my job to know things."

I slide him a guarded look. Being the Regent's right-hand man, he must know plenty of things. But I keep my questions and comments to myself.

The street starts to curve around. I notice there aren't any side streets leading off, but just the narrow spaces between buildings.

"Where do those alleyways lead to?"

Reddik looks to where I've pointed. "They lead to the first ward." When he sees my confused expression, he explains. "The city is laid out in three separate wards. Those alleyways lead into the first ward, the place where the citizens of Pynth dwell. They have their own streets and courtyards—a safe haven of sorts. The pathway we find ourselves in now is in the second ward. This is where all the merchants have their shops, providing everything for the people."

"I see. So where's the third ward?"

"The third ward is tucked between the outer wall and the second ward. There you will find the training grounds for our soldiers."

"It is one of the many brilliant designs of the Western Kingdom," the Regent chimes in. "This design protects the people. The wall was built after your departure; it helps security even more. If an army comes into this city, they will have a hard time getting through a wall as well as two other wards to reach our people. Even the road up to the castle bypasses the first ward."

"I don't remember reading about these wards in my studies."

I look back to where Amah is lagging behind. She's deep

in her own thoughts. So I drop back and ride next to her, leaving the men to themselves.

"Everything okay?" I ask.

"Of course, En Oli. Being here brings back many memories. I find myself going back in time."

"From when you lived at the Temple?"

"Yes."

"What about the Willow Sisters?"

Amah's lips purse together, but she stays silent.

"Can you tell me something of their beliefs?" I press.

Amah pretends to brush something off her sleeve, then adjusts her hands neatly on the horn of her saddle.

"I have always kept my religious beliefs to myself. Always. In the Tar Islands where I was born, there was no Maker. We believed that people always existed, having come forth from the very soil we worked.

When the Willow Sisters ventured to our islands, they were cast out, and told never to return. Just before that, I'd lost my parents to the plague. I was left starving in the streets. I was nothing but bones. The Sisters took me in the under cover of darkness before the slave masters could find me. They brought me back with them on their ship. I thank them now for saving me from the slave lands of Tar, but back then I knew only hate for what they believed in.

It took years for them to convince me of the truth of their Maker and his Guardians that protected the four kingdoms of Erets. I learned that when the magic disappeared, and the people prayed to Maker Adon, they begged him to send down the Guardians once again and bless the four kingdoms. But the Maker has never responded, nor has he sent his Guardians.

Soon the people lost hope. They started to rebuild their world and put their faith in men, and in the kings who ruled them. But not everyone forgot the Maker and all he'd done for them. The Willow Sisters have remained faithful all these years, and they remain here in the Temple, continuing to pray and live in truth, wisdom, strength, and love. Their mission is to awaken in others the belief that magic will return, to prove that the Maker listens and loves us after all."

"So is this what you believe now?"

Her mouth turns down. "I believe in the Maker. It makes more sense than rising up from the dirt. But when I left the Temple, I was challenged and it drove doubt inside me. For such a long time after, I trusted only myself. But now I see your gift, I see the heart that lies behind it, and I feel a bud of hope growing inside me. I find myself praying once again for your safety."

This is the most I've ever heard of Amah's life. I hope to hear more, but silence stretches on and my hope is in vain. Only the sounds of heartened people fill the air.

When the crowd's excitement begins to soften, I notice the road has opened up into a large grassy courtyard. And then I see it—Willow Round. I feel exultation surge through me.

So many times Amah has told me of this sacred place. She might have avoided telling me about inside the Temple, but she was never discouraged from speaking of the beating heart of Pynth, known to everyone as The Willow.

The courtyard is a vast grassy space, manicured to perfection. A large ancient willow tree stands at its center. Only the bones of the tree can be seen; the buds are long gone. But the weeping white branches look beautiful in their ancient ways, still capturing the magic they once had.

Cool air breezes through, and I realize how quiet it has become. The stillness of the people here brings to mind statues; only these statues breathe and wait in anticipation. Leading our horses around The Willow, we join Regent Grif and Reddik at the base of the Temple.

The Temple is of moderate size, stretching up just five stories, with a top floor fully exposed in glass. The stark white marble is covered with thick green vines, as if the Temple has grown straight up from the ground. A wide archway extends out over the marble steps; these lead to two wooden doors, rounded at the top.

"It's unbelievable," I exclaim.

The Temple doors open, and women in lavender robes come out in single file, breaking away to either side as they reach the bottom. We wait in silence as over a hundred Willow Sisters fill Willow Round. A last Willow Sister stands yet at the doors. She wears an elaborate robe with simple gold designs.

"That is Prelate Rishima," Amah informs me. "She is the leader of the Sisters."

We all dismount and proceed across Willow Round, the thick grass absorbing our weight. We stop when we reach a stone path at the base of the Temple.

My gift hums beneath my skin, as if it senses the lost touch of magic, as if it knows this place. The wind dances softly, sending my hair gently about. Even though I've never been here, I feel the comfort of home.

The Prelate opens her arms. "Welcome, Your Royal Highness, Princess Livia, future queen of the people. We are honored to have you here at Guardian Pynth's Temple."

In that moment, everyone kneels down and bows their heads. Like a subtle flutter in the wind, a softly-voiced song comes from the Sisters. I can't quite make it out. That is until the people join in.

"O*H*' *ring the bell, sweet Queen Bellflower*
  An heir will hear your call
  Ring, ring, my Queen Bellflower
  Her touch shall save us all.

"O*H*' *ring the bell, sweet Queen Bellflower*

Her life is yours forevermore
Ring, ring, my Queen Bellflower
We'll love you evermore."

THE WORDS ARE FAMILIAR. It's a song written down in one of the many books on Amah's shelves, back in the pines. It is said to have been a popular medley a long time ago, and it's taught to all the children. The rest of the song speaks of Queen Bellflower's journey. I have always found its message sad—that loss of her magic.

I'm shocked to hear them singing her words to me, linking me to the most powerful queen of old. Prelate Rishima stands, and motions me to join her. I take my dress in my hand, and ascend the stairs. The sisters rise as I pass by, and follow us back inside the Temple.

I'm in a large circular room that has walls lined with alcoves, each with a short pillar that holds a metal brazier with small orange flames burning in its center. At the far end of the room, a large statue of Guardian Pynth stands, an altar set before him.

I follow the Prelate up more steps at the western end of the room. The other sisters do not follow; instead they go to kneel near the statue. When I glance to my caretaker, her expression is grim.

"I'm under the impression," the Prelate probes, "that you are here to speak with Scholar Eli?" Her heavy-lidded eyes peer intently into mine. She has done nothing to warrant any fear, but her presence alone makes me slightly tremble.

"Y...yes. He asked me to come visit him."

She clasps her hands together and nods knowingly.

"Good, good. Scholar Eli has studied the magical books his whole life. I'm sure he'll be able to help you learn in no time. Just know this, the Willow Sisters take all this very seriously. We have devoted our lives in service to Maker Adon, and we will not tolerate any form of blasphemy."

My brows snap up. "Oh! I would never, Prelate Rishima. I am beyond curious to know everything and willing to embrace it all."

Her eyes narrow down for only a moment. "I'm glad to hear that, princess. There are those who have lost faith, and it's our job to guide them back to see the truth."

It happens so fast, I could've imagined it, but I swear the Prelate glances towards Amah before her eyes return to me.

"You will find Scholar Eli in here. If you find you are in need of anything, do not hesitate to call."

Prelate Rishima bows her head.

"The rest of you may follow me."

"Excuse me?" Amah asks quickly.

"Only those who are royal, or Sisters of the Temple may enter. None of you qualify. You should know that, Amah." The Prelate's words are crisp and to the point.

I am shocked, and look to my uncle. I wasn't aware this was the plan. Before Amah can offer a retort, the Regent gives her a stern look, then responds to the Prelate.

"I am glad to join you, Prelate. However, I would ask if Reddik might stand just outside the door. You can understand how cautious we must be with Livia's return."

"Of course, Regent Grif."

I watch them follow after her, Amah's face red with anger. Reddik takes up his position next to the door. I'm about to say something, but he shakes his head, and motions me to go inside. I can't help but feel something's amiss.

I pass through the thick wooden door frame, and enter into a massive domed-shaped room, complete with a clear glass ceiling. I stare wide-eyed at the thousands upon thousands of books stacked in neat rows, all arranged in an orderly fashion. Amah had only a single bookshelf in our cottage. This is well beyond that, and so much more. Each one of these books has to hold its own world of wonders and answers to long held questions about life.

The morning light that shines down through the glass ceiling shows me everything. I scan the room as fast as I can, trying to take it all in. I go to the nearest shelf and run my fingers along the spines of the books. They smell old and dry —wisdom on paper.

"Ah, Princess Livia."

An old man comes out from behind one of the shelves, hunched over, his gait slow.

"Scholar Eli."

A smile touches his lips. "It is I. I can see that you are pleased by what you see?"

"Oh, yes! I've never seen so many books before. I could get lost for days and months in here, trying to read them all."

"Or years." Scholar Eli chuckles at his own joke. "Come. I have gathered some books that might interest you the most."

I follow him through the maze of shelves to a heavy oak table. Three books are laid out open, displaying their contents.

"What do you know of the magic of old?"

"I know what the four gifts are, and how Queen Bell-flower was the first and last to have more than one."

Scholar Eli frowns. "I'm surprised Amah didn't share everything with you. Especially since she spent most of her life here at the Temple. No matter, no matter. I will share with you what I know to be a basic explanation." He rubs his hands together, and has an excited twinkle in his eyes.

"Maker Adon claimed this land, dividing it into four king-doms. He sent out four of his finest Guardians, and let them build up their own unique lands. Icewyn built up the ice lands in the North. Dryden pushed rock around in his kingdom to form mountains in the East. Acadia loved only himself, and made in the South only a single temple in the desert lands. And, of course, there is Pynth—our Guardian of the West. His love for nature is what makes our kingdom thrive more over the rest.

After a time, Maker Adon called back his Guardians. It was time for men to govern the land. The Guardians each left a single unique gift with a ruler of their choosing. This ruler was the only one left in the kingdom who was able to wield the Guardian's magic. Until the rulers bore children, then came magic to their children's children, so forth."

"So there were multiple people at one time that had the gift?"

"Yes. But only direct descendants. Now the gift of these others wasn't as strong as that of the main ruler. In fact, their recovery time after using the gift was much longer."

I stand up straighter. "Recovery time?"

Scholar Eli pulls out a chair. "Here, sit."

He flips through the pages of the first book, and points to the bottom of the page.

Strength is taken from whomever uses the Guardian's gift. The one who holds the one true power inherits the strength of the one before. This in turn makes them stronger than they had been, and allows them to recover faster. But anyone with the gift must be wary of using it, for the magic will claim them, bonding to their soul.

"Have you experienced this bonding?" Eli asks.

I think back to the intense headache from healing Oliver.

"I think so. Is this bad?"

"No, it's not bad. It's wonderful! You are the one true holder of Pynth's gift."

"What about my sister?"

"She will not be as strong as you. That's if she has the same gift as you. Do we know what gift your sister acquired?"

I lean back in my chair. "No. I actually don't know anything about her."

While Scholar Eli sits and ponders for a bit, I lean forward and see the second book has the words *Queen Bellflower* on the top page.

"The Willow Sisters sang a portion of Queen Bellflower's song to me on my arrival," I say. "Do you know why?"

"The question is, princess, do *you* know why? What part of the song did they sing?"

"*An heir will hear your call, her touch shall save us all.*"

"Yes. Do you see now? This song has been sung for centuries, speaking its own prophecy. The Willow Sisters were told when you arrived in the city that you bore the violet eyes of our Guardian Pynth. They knew you were the one."

"The one? You mean this song is the prophecy?"

"Not the prophecy the Eastern King received, but it is a prophecy nonetheless."

"So they think I'm the one to bring back all magic?"

"Not only magic, but life! You have the gift of healing. So many can benefit from just a touch and a thought from you. It changes everything."

Trying not to let his words overwhelm me, I flip through more of the pages. I stop when I stumble upon a colorful picture of a young woman dressed in violet robes. Her face is smooth and slender, with long raven locks like my own. When I see the bright violet shade of her eyes, it feels like I'm looking into a mirror. I look below the picture.

"Queen Bellflower? Why, I look exactly like her!" I exclaim.

Scholar Eli laughs. "Which makes their singing the song to you even more haunting."

I spend the next hour pouring over passages of Queen Bellflower. While I grew up reading about her, this additional information is in more depth.

She was named after the brightest violet flower in the Western Kingdom. A flower that went extinct shortly after her disappearance. It is known to have been made into a healing elixir that was sold to the other kingdoms.

I read other passages that proclaim her the youngest Western queen to ever rule. Sixteen—the same age I am now.

They say she never married, but had a lover. Even when she became pregnant, the father never stepped forward, and she never uttered a word of who he was.

Her own son was born sick, and he became deathly ill. She found that her spark of magic could not heal the one person who meant the world to her. Desperate, she traveled to the only kingdom that dabbled in the dark magic forbidden in her own land—the kingdom of the Enchanter. When Guardian Acadia left his gift of invisibility, he also left behind a book of spells. It allowed his chosen one to live forever—as long as he remained inside the Temple.

The Enchanter agreed to heal her child, but only if she would sacrifice her gifts. Desperate—she did.

Queen Bellflower traveled back home a mortal, only to discover at the end of her long journey that the very magic she had sacrificed was entirely gone. All the kingdoms were stripped of their magic. When the gift was extracted from the queen, it took out magic from its very roots.

The Northern and Eastern Kingdoms were furious, as well as the queen's own people. They commanded her to return to the Enchanter, and demand back the magic for their lands.

For weeks she was gone, then weeks became months, and months turned into years. Finally everyone knew she would never return—and she never did.

The council stood in for the queen, doing their best to live without magic—but it wasn't the same. The queen's child grew up, and when he came of age the people hoped the magic would return in him, but it never did.

But the new king, having grown up without the magic, took control of his sullen people and encouraged them to be fruitful once again. He grew to hate the Enchanter, and reinforced the law forbidding anyone from having dealings with that devious man, making sure that with even a whisper of his name, one would become cursed.

The people loved their king and kept his commands. They put the thought of magic behind them. But the people never truly forgot, and they continued to hope the magic would return one day.

17

VERA

"Have you ever been sent on a mission?"

Captain Leech has found me sitting alone in front of a small fire, and decided to join me.

"I have not. Usually the captains and commanders are kept from those missions. It's curious the king sent Bellek out when he did. I have a feeling this war is the beginning of many new things to come."

"He puts too much faith in my gift. I know what he expects of me. I can only hope I'm able to carry it out."

"What you did at The Wall reflects what is yet to come. It was powerful watching it unfold, and it will give the commander of the Violet Guard something to fear."

I pick up a twig and throw it in the flames.

"What do you know about their guard?" I ask.

"I know they have thousands more men than we do. Commander Barrett hasn't been leading them long. He is young, but he is a sharp-witted bastard. I had the chance to meet him once, when he was doing inspections at The Wall. For years we had been trying to infiltrate them, and had succeeded with a good number of men. In just one visit, he rooted out all of our assassins, and put them to death on the spot. He isn't afraid of us, and that is something to watch out for."

"What about the Regent?"

"He's a Northern Prince, fifth in line for the throne. He is known as a great soldier in his land, and it was the reason he was sent to help govern the West. For so many years the North and West have been allied to keep us behind The Wall. But I know the Regent's weakness."

"What's that?"

Leech shakes his head uncomfortably. "I won't say. But his right-hand man keeps him in check well enough for him not to break. That man is a Northern Shadow—an elite guard and advisor in the North. He has saved the Regent's life a time or two. You would never know upon meeting him, but he handles plenty of unpleasantries in the dark."

"How do you know so much about them?"

"Commander Bellek keeps us captains in the know about everything. We study their men in any way we can. No knowledge is lost knowledge."

"So why doesn't the Regent become king? He has governed there for sixteen years now. What stops him from taking the throne?"

Leech presses his lips together, and looks around.

"The one thing the Maker declared in all the kingdoms was that only the descendants of the Guardian's chosen one can rule. This is why the king holds so tightly to you. He must keep you from just walking over there and placing the crown on your head."

Leech clamps his mouth shut, realizing he's said too much.

"Am I the next in line? Is there truly no one else?" I think of the girl in the golden mirror. "Do I have relatives that I don't know about?"

"You sure are a curious commander." Ryker comes from behind us, sitting down next to Leech.

I pin him with a frosty glare. "Mind your business, *Captain*."

"You are my business, *Commander*."

"Oh, Ryker, give her a break. She needs to know what we are up against. Would you have her go in blind?" Leech retorts.

"Of course not. But what does the Western throne have to do with leading our men to victory?"

Leech furrows his brow, but doesn't respond. I take his lead, and do my best to ignore Ryker. He can only still be upset about King Kgar's decision to make me Commander instead of him. I refuse to let him get under my skin.

Ryker stands up to leave. "Oh, Commander. A messenger showed up for you. He awaits you in your tent."

When he turns to leave, Leech nervously glances my way.

"You need me to come with you?"

I shake my head. "No, that would only be worse."

Especially if it's who I think it is.

BRUCE IS STANDING THERE with his hands behind his back. Between him and the king, they both have made my life a living hell. With the king protected by the Scree's contract, I am guessing he can afford to let his elite assassin travel many miles away from him.

He meets my defiant glare. I will always hate this man who stole me away from my parents' grasp and brought me to a nightmarish fate.

"I was informed you had a message from the king."

Bruce brings a box out from behind his back, and sets it on a table nearby, then hands me a sealed scroll. I swiftly take it from him and nonchalantly step back. I crack the seal and unfurl the message.

My Vera, I hope this message finds you closer to achieving my victory. I have decided to allow Bruce to travel with you, to handle some unfinished business of mine. He brings with him a reminder from me to you on what will happen if you try to stop him or betray me. The Scree wasn't here to save your love this time around. Enjoy.

King Kgar

My blood runs cold as I glance over to the box. I hesitantly go over, and open the lid. A severed hand is lying inside. I cover my mouth. Even now, Marcus continues to bleed for me. I shake my head, an anger burning inside me. I look to Bruce. I could kill him now, and the king would never know.

I ignite my gift over my body, and bring a single thought to my mind. But nothing happens. I try again. Nothing. Looking down to my hands, I'm confused. I feel the hum over my entire body. Why isn't it working?

Bruce reaches inside the collar of his threads and pulls out a chain hanging around his neck with a bluish red stone hanging down. He sways it in front of me. Whatever it is, it mutes my gift. Seeing that I understand, he places it back underneath his threads, and walks out from my tent.

Shit.

"HOLY HELL, I'M RUINED."

"I still can't believe you continued seeing Marcus." Murrow spits out his disgust. I'd gone in search of my friends shortly after dismissing Bruce. They have always known of Marcus, but never said much about him and me. Nate always gets quiet whenever Marcus is mentioned, and always refuses to give an opinion of him. I made the mistake of asking once, and his sneer was enough for me to not ask again.

"Forget about Marcus. What about the fact that Bruce can deflect my gift?" I ask.

They glance to one another, sharing a look.

"What?"

"Vera, we don't know anything of the magic," Nate answers. "We know only to fear it, though no one will admit it." The others agree. "But I would put nothing past King Kgar to dabble in things that shouldn't be dabbled in."

We spend the next few minutes staring into the fire, before I excuse myself to lie down in my tent. It seems no one can really tell me anything.

I lead my assassins blindly, trusting a king who has abused me my whole life. But if what Leech said is true, about the throne being mine in the West, why haven't my people come to rescue me? What has kept the most powerful kingdom from coming to take me out of the Eastern King's clutches?

I feel suddenly stupid for thinking I could ever live in the West. Why would I even want to live with people who've done nothing to help me? These thousands of assassins have had my back more than anyone else in all the other kingdoms. Screw the king and his mad plans; I will take the West for my men and give them what they deserve. It's the only thing I can control for myself.

18

LIVIA

SCHOLAR ELI INTRODUCES many books to me over the next few days. I find it interesting how the healing gift is able to sustain the lives of kings and queens, extending their rule. This has meant they've been able to have many more children, who've also inherited the Guardian's gift.

When I ask Scholar Eli about it, he says there were over a hundred descendants who had the gift at one time. Status determined the strength of their gift. The oldest could heal an entire village in one day, while the youngest could only mend minor cuts and bruises.

However, I search in vain to uncover anything on the golden mirror. No mention of strange dreams or the visitation of a separate world can be found in anything I read.

These last two nights I've stood again in front of the golden mirror, seeing but unable to communicate with my sister. I try to read her lips when she speaks, but it is near to impossible to piece it all together. It is beyond frustrating. Especially since I know the Silent Watchers are marching this way. Does she know about me? Does she know she is about to kill her own people?

"It will be curious to see if any of the lost plants and beasts will return now that the balance of magic has awoken," Scholar Eli proclaims.

I look over and see a colorful painting of a Shicat, a magical creature that resembles a small cream-colored house cat with long pointy ears, tipped black. Small black spots cover a Shicat's legs and paws, making it easier to distinguish between these beautiful creatures. And with the simple sound of their purr, they can put you into a deep slumber.

"Oh, I hope so."

Eli turns the page to show a ferocious Berwhol. The creature is the size of two giant bears put together, with a long, golden horn upon its head.

"Or perhaps, maybe not all of them need to come back," I quickly add.

"We can only hope they don't all come back, princess. We are lucky only the Keppers survived by staying in the mountains. But the plant life would be more than welcomed. I know your mother would have loved it."

"What do you mean?"

"Queen Kyra loved plant life. She was always freshening the castle with all sorts of beautiful flowers. Your father even had a garden made for her very own."

I remember when Uncle Grif told me of the garden she'd had in the North. A gentle smile graces my lips.

"Scholar Eli, can I ask you something?"

The light from above illuminates his tired, worn face. "But, of course."

"Have you ever come across anything about a golden mirror?"

His expression turns suspicious. He snaps the book in front of him closed, giving me his undivided attention.

"How do you know about this golden mirror?"

"I overheard someone mention it, and it sounded interesting," I lie.

I know he can see straight through me, but his experience dances on his lips, and he proceeds to share his knowledge.

"The golden mirror is an ancient piece of magic. It was used many, many years ago; it was a magical object given to the first king. It is said that a king could communicate through it, that time did not exist when he used it. The golden mirror was stolen after Queen Bellflower's disappearance. A war almost broke out because of the theft, as the alliances between the kingdoms were already fragile with the magic gone, but the rulers decided it wasn't worth destroying the kingdoms over it. No one ever found it, and no one has seen it since."

"How does one communicate through it?"

"I am unsure, princess. There isn't much information about the lost mirror. The mirror is now regarded as a myth, something that never existed."

I slump back in my chair. I need to know how to talk to Vera.

I SPEND the rest of the morning reading until my eyes are crossed and won't function any longer. The moment Scholar Eli begins nodding off, I quietly leave.

I find Reddik standing outside the library, exactly where I leave him every day, and we leave the Temple. The streets are full of people gathering supplies for the days to come. The Regent sent word out earlier this week for the people of Pynth to prepare for war. When I asked him about it, he said the Silent Watchers have broken through the northern wall. But when he told me of the casualties and the involvement of my sister, that left me feeling devastated. If I don't talk to her soon, it will be harder than ever to let her return.

"You know, princess, the Temple isn't going anywhere anytime soon. You have plenty of time to discover and learn about this lost magic. Surely there are other things you want to do?"

Reddik has taken it upon himself to promise to escort me to the Temple whenever I want to go. Amah has been more than happy not to return since our first visit. Whatever happened those many years ago continues to leave a bitter taste in her mouth.

"The more I know about what I can do, the better for our people," I reply. "That is where I need to focus. I must help any way I can."

"Spoken like a true queen." He dips his head, and his mouth curves up in a smile.

I have been grateful for Reddik's companionship, and I find that I enjoy his company more than I probably should. I wish I had someone I could share these thoughts with. Like a sister. I breathe in deep.

"You all right, princess?"

"Just thinking about Vera."

Reddik's jaw tightens. "I understand."

The way he responds unnerves me. It's as if he finds it to be Vera's fault that King Kgar's army of assassins is coming this way.

"Do you?" I say defensively. "I don't see anyone else caring about her."

The sharpness of my words catches him off guard, and his face softens.

"I know you—"

A shout of warning cuts him off.

We both glance ahead, just as an arrow whizzes past Reddik's head. Two burly men wearing bright clothing are standing in our path. One stands ready with his sword, while the other nocks another arrow.

The crowd around us disperses into chaos, erupting into screams. Reddik pulls his horse in front of Rosie as the second arrow is released.

His horse rears up, releasing a painful cry. Reddik is thrown, and his stallion gallops off past the men. I quickly dismount, going to Reddik's side, but he's up before I reach him and brandishing his sword.

"Run back to the Temple, princess." I shake my head, but he responds sternly. "Now! Go!"

I run back to Rosie with my heart pounding. I'm not fond of the idea of leaving Reddik behind. A clashing of swords causes me to turn back. Instead of witnessing a sword fight, I see the archer sprinting towards me. I hurry and grab Rosie's saddle to hoist myself up, but I'm not fast enough and I'm yanked roughly back.

I grab hold of his arm to pry him off of me. The moment my fingers touch his flesh, a prickling sensation rumbles deep inside my chest. Unknowingly, I release an unfamiliar gift, like a bolt of lightning escaping a storm. The burly man seizes, collapsing to the ground. I look aghast at my hands— confused and somewhat frightened. What did I just do?

The chiming of bells sounds off in the distance. I stare at the dead man at my feet. The size of him reminds me of the assassin in the Black Pines. The numbness of shock settles over me, and I can't move. These two men are Silent Watchers.

My head whips up. A bright light reflects off Reddik's opponent's bald head. Sweat trickles down the bald head, landing in his overly bushy eyebrows. His eyes shift from Reddik to me. I always thought they wore masks; but these men do not.

Recognition flashes across his face. But is quickly extinguished when he must block Reddik's advance. With deadly speed, he arcs his blade out. Time slows as I watch blood spray out from Reddik's side. I hear someone scream, but realize it's the sound of my own cry.

Hooves thunder ahead of us. The standing assassin glances behind him and then back to me. He steps over a fallen Reddik and then towards me. But his steps freeze when he sees the dead assassin at my feet. He curses under his breath. "Damn it. Just like your sister."

"Do you know her?" I ask desperately.

His scowl deepens before dashing past me to flee the scene. The Violet Guard rein in, frantically surveying my surroundings. I yell at the one in the lead, and point behind me. "Hurry, he went that way. Bring him back alive!"

They ride on after him, and I rush to Reddik's side where he lies in a pool of his own blood. Kneeling down I ignore the wetness already seeping through my dress. I thrust my hand through the slit in his leather armor, trying to ignore the tears streaming down my face and place my hand on his wound.

I close my eyes.

Immediately, I notice his pulse is thready and weakening. I choke back my fear, as I feel the seriousness of his injury. My gift swiftly steadies his heartbeat and maintains his blood pressure as I focus on his fatal wound. I promptly bring everything together, mending him back, until there is only a fine line from my finished work noticeable. I send one last final current, smoothing out his skin.

When I open my eyes, I see Reddik sitting up. He pats his side, trying to feel the gash he knows was just there. But he finds it mended. He turns to face me, and is mere inches from me. I feel his breath on my face. My heart flickers as our eyes lock. His eyes shift down to my lips, and then back up. I wonder what it would be like to feel his lips on mine.

An awareness seeps into Reddik's face. "The bells!"

Hurriedly, he pushes himself up, and brings me up with him.

Confused, I ask, "What does it mean?"

"We have two bells. One's for a prison break, the other's for castle breech."

"Which one is this?"

"Castle breech."

Realization crosses over my face. Reddik mounts quickly onto Rosie, pulling me up behind him. He takes note of the dead assassin, but he doesn't say anything. As I hold him tight around his waist, he sends Rosie flying through the streets, giving those in the way only moments to move. I can only hope he doesn't ask me what I've done.

When we reach the stables, Oliver is there to fill us in. "They were wearing our soldiers' uniforms. No one thought anything of it when they passed on through."

"Who did they target, Oliver?"

"Regent Grif," he regretfully informs us.

I take off running, with Reddik fast on my heels. Servants jump out of the way as we run through the castle. When we reach the Regent's chambers, Amah is pacing outside his doors. She rushes over when she sees us.

"Oh, En Oli! I'm glad you're okay." She takes in my disheveled appearance, and the blood covering my dress. "What in Maker's name happened to the two of you?"

"We were attacked," Reddik explains, "by two Silent Watchers on our way back from the Temple."

"And the assassins? What happened to them?" she asks.

Reddik gives me a sidelong glance. "One is dead, the other is being chased down by our guards."

"Good," Amah answers with a curt nod.

"Is the Regent all right?" I finally ask.

"He'll be fine. But there's a poisoned arrow lodged in his shoulder. The healers are working on him now."

We all turn when we hear yelling coming from inside.

"What do you mean you can't do anything more? What is the point of having you, if you can't do your job!" This comes from Lady Ella.

A softer voice responds. "He will be fine, Lady Ella. The poison will work itself out with time."

"Well, thank goodness! The princess is lucky my husband

didn't rat her out. I would have blabbed out anything to save my own life."

Reddik and Amah look to me, and my cheeks warm. Amah steps past me and enters the Regent's chambers.

"Well, then it's a good thing you were not the one being questioned," Amah snaps.

Lady Ella gasps, before placing a nasty scowl on her face. "Who are you to speak to me that way?" I step out from behind Amah, and my aunt's eyes widen. "Princess Livia!" Her expression softens. "I only meant that I could never be that brave."

Amah scoffs. "No, you didn't. I know exactly what you meant, and you will be well advised to keep in mind who Livia actually is to you."

Lady Ella's nostrils flare. "I will not be treated so rudely!"

The Regent groans from his bed, but before Amah can unleash her fury, my aunt rushes to my uncle's side, and takes his hand. "It's okay, my love. The healers say you only need to rest."

Amah pulls me forward. "Go and heal him." Her hand shoos me forward and I go to my uncle without making eye contact with my aunt, now that I'm under the impression she'd like me dead.

I place my hand on my uncle's shoulder, and am surprised by how hot he feels. I close my eyes, and am alarmed when I see black flecks within the red hue around his shoulder. I reach out and graze the injury with my mind, and a sharp pain shoots through me. Backing off, I can taste the bitterness of the toxin. I push out again, concentrating my gift to go through the toxic barrier. I ignore the pain it causes me, and successfully break through. I sweep away the poison, and smooth the red to a calming golden hue.

Uncle Grif squeezes my hand, and I open my eyes. "Amazing," he says.

Lady Ella looks from one to the other of us, her brow furrowing in confusion.

"Without even looking, I know I'm healed," Uncle Grif says. "Livia, your gift is incredible."

I smile and sneak a glance to Reddik. He steps forward and reports to the Regent the events we encountered.

"I'm glad you both are all right. I'll be very much interested in meeting this assassin," the Regent says.

"The assassin is King Kgar's uncle."

"Bellek?" Amah huffs out.

Regent Grif frowns. "Are you sure, Reddik?"

"I would never forget the face of the commanding officer of those most feared assassins."

"Why would he be here now, and not with his army?"

Silence fills the room until a knock comes at the door. A messenger enters and waits to be heard.

"Speak," Regent Grif gruffs.

"The assassin in the city has been captured, sire. He is being taken to the dungeon as we speak."

Regent Grif waves his hand dismissively, and the lad leaves. Amah watches him, and I see the wheels turning in her head. "If I may excuse myself, there are some things I must attend to." My uncle nods, and Amah gives me a half-smile before leaving me behind.

"Reddik, I think it's time we have Princess Livia go to one of our trainers. It would be in her best interest to be able to defend herself. Today was too close a call, and with war on our doorstep—well, I think it would be helpful."

"Agreed, sir."

"Good. Now if you both don't mind, I need to have a word with my wife."

Lady Ella's mouth twists into a forced smile. Not wanting to be anywhere near this conversation, I am the first to turn to leave.

. . .

WHEN THE DOORS open to the training room, my mouth curves up in a pleasant grin.

"Wow."

The vast space is hollowed out of mountainous rock. My head goes every which way, trying to soak it all in. Guards are scattered everywhere, practicing their skills, and a faint hint of sweat is in the air.

One whole side of the room juts out to resemble a mountain, allowing soldiers to practice scaling a wall. I can barely make out the guard at the top. The danger is daunting, and I know it takes a lot of nerve to attempt something so dangerous.

"Well, it seems your trainer is busy at the moment," Reddik says as he peers up at the same guard.

"Is that him?"

"His name is Cam, and he's a force to be reckoned with. I warn you, he'll not go easy on you."

I continue watching Cam as he swings himself from one ledge to the next. My breath catches when one of his hands slips and he's left dangling by the tips of the fingers of one hand. He regains his position, and resumes making his way down.

I blow air out from my lungs, and Reddik laughs.

"Don't worry, he won't be having you do anything crazy. Just learning to handle a blade."

He guides me over to a rack holding an array of weapons. I spot a quiver full of arrows, and run my fingers along one's fletching.

"Do you shoot?" he asks.

"Since I was seven. It saddens me that I left my bow behind in Kale. I miss the feel of the release."

"You want to take this one for a go?"

"I would love to!"

I snatch up the quiver of arrows and the bow leaning next

to it. Hooking the strap over my shoulder, I follow Reddik to the targets nearby.

I align my body with a target, and nock my first arrow. I release it, and it hits dead center. Reddik lifts a brow, clearly impressed. I set the next, and release arrow after arrow, letting my muscles and body take over.

The tension in my body begins to release. I let my mind get lost in the precision of my skill, allowing all my arrows to hit their mark. I am happy here in this moment.

Releasing my last arrow, someone starts clapping behind me. I turn and see the mountain climbing man—Cam. He is a tall guard with dark hair and enormous shoulders. He looks like the sort of man you would threaten someone with.

"Princess Livia, this is Cam."

Cam bows his head. "Your Royal Highness. That is quite the shot you have there. You could give our finest archers a lesson."

I smile at his compliment. "Thank you. I regret to say, though, that I'm not as skilled with a blade."

"Oh, I'll get you there with a blade before you know it. Actually, you might not want to see a blade ever again when I'm through with you, but you'll know how to wield it."

"Don't be scaring her, Cam. She's already had an eventful day."

"No, it's okay, Reddik. I need to learn it, and I can take whatever Cam dishes out to me." Cam looks impressed as he glances at Reddik. I love how my confidence is beginning to grow. Maybe I can be who they need me to be after all.

Cam works me hard for the next hour, having me practice with a wooden stick. He goes over my footwork until my muscles are on fire. Towards the end I feel I've grasped the concept, and gift him a smile when he says I look promising.

Reddik tries hard not to laugh as he escorts me back to my chambers.

"You look like you are going to die," he says.

"Well, you would, too, if your muscles were never worked that way before!"

"Okay, okay, I'm sorry. I promise tomorrow will be easier."

"Liar."

Reddik laughs. "You're smart, princess. But just so you know, Cam knows what he's doing. Trust him, and he'll get you to where you need to be."

We arrive to my chambers. "I hope so."

The last thing I see before closing my door is Reddik's quirky grin. And there isn't a doubt in my mind how much he means to me.

19

GOLDEN MIRROR

A GOLDEN MIRROR standing in time; a looking glass without reflection; everything full of mystery and frustration.

Livia stares into the golden mirror.

And at her sister.

She refuses to go another night without communication. Walking around the mirror, Livia scours the intricate details, looking for anything that might explain the workings of this magical object.

Vera just observes. It seems like the other girl is a prisoner, trapped and desperate to get out. Vera has lost count of all the times her dreams have brought her to this same scenario, time and time again. She is growing tired of the monotonous routine.

Vera has tried to talk to the girl many times, but to no avail. Vera can hear nothing the other says. So she stares in silence at the girl who looks just like herself, on who seems to be trying to escape a cage. Maybe, it is an image of her own mind, after all.

· · ·

THEN SOMETHING HAPPENS that changes the dynamic of their frustrating dreams.

LIVIA STEPS BACK in front of the mirror. Her brow puckers with unrelenting determination. Reaching out with her hand, she touches the shiny surface of the mirror.

A strong wind blasts out at her from the mirror, spiraling her hair behind her. She watches as her sister's eyes widen.

Livia: *Hello? Can you hear me?*

She sees her sister nod.

Livia points to Vera, then to her own hand touching the mirror; she motions Vera to touch the mirror. She anxiously watches Vera reach out and touch the glass. A gust of wind blows Vera's hair back the same as it did Livia's.

Livia: *Can you hear me?*

Vera: *Yes.*

The tension and frustration, like a wall, collapses down around Livia. As much as she tries to hold it in, she can't. A tear escapes down her cheek. She can finally talk to her sister.

Livia: *Do you know who I am?*

Vera's brows knit together.

Vera: *Are you me?*

Livia: *I am your sister.*

Vera: *That can't be possible.*

Livia: *It's the truth. Our parents were murdered. I was able to escape, but you were taken. Has no one told you?*

Vera knows this girl is not her sister. Kgar never hesitates to shove in her face the horrors of her life. This is something the king would not hide from her. It only makes sense that this girl in this mirror, or cage, is speaking what she can only wish to be the truth. Nothing else.

Livia: *Look, you are coming to Pynth with an army of assassins. You must stop them. The people of Pynth are yours, just as they are mine. You have to believe me.*

Vera: *They are not my people. If they were, then why have they never come for me? They don't deserve my pity.*

Livia shakes her head in frustration. Time will run out before she can convince Vera otherwise. Something has to be done to change her perspective.

Livia: *Are you at least being treated well?*

Vera: *I am an assassin. Living free of pain is not a luxury I get to enjoy.*

Livia: *Surely you want better for yourself. I can offer you protection, and you can have the luxury of peace. I can help you.*

Vera: *There is no such thing as peace. You are only a thought in my head, a crazy idea I once dreamt of as a child. You're a trick of my mind, nothing more. If you were my sister, I would've been told.*

Livia: *Please believe me.*

Vera: *I tire of this game.*

Vera takes her hand off from the glass, and steps back into the fog.

20

VERA

THE NEXT DAY we ride with urgency to stay warm. Icy air comes off the snow that fell overnight. The cold clings to everything, wrapping around our cloaks, trying to find a way inside to suck out our warmth.

The country is gradually flattening, the woods growing sparser each hour. In a day's time, we will be close enough to Pynth to make our final camp. The arrival will be good for the subdued assassins, who are used to training day in and day out. I sense their restlessness.

Occasionally, I bark an order, and the entire company makes a gradual change in direction. It isn't much, considering our route is straight southwest. With thousands of men, it's barely noticeable anyways, but it keeps them alert.

Since this morning, I've remained in my own mind, riding ahead of the captains just to keep my thoughts to myself. I can't stop thinking about the mystery girl on the other side of the golden mirror. It's as if she is trying to ensnare me in a trap.

No matter how many times I try to convince myself she is some fabrication of a childhood dream, I can't help but think she is real. While she looks identical to me, her expressions and tone of voice are someone else entirely.

A Kepper screeches somewhere behind us, and its call sends a chill down my spine. It seems the soldiers are not the only ones restless. I turn to Leech. "Can you not keep those beasts quiet, captain?"

He brings his light-coated horse up next to mine, smiling apologetically. "I'm afraid not, Commander. You look tired; do you need to get some rest?"

"Rest? Ha! What's that?"

Leech chuckles. "This will be a battle of the elite, Commander. Our chances are quite good. And our men know better than to show any weakness even if they should feel your doubt. You have a force behind you that's not afraid to fight to the very end."

I nod in response.

WHEN THE SUN begins sinking rapidly below the horizon, I call the assassins to a halt. We settle down seconds before being shrouded in night. Soon those not on watch are around the campfires drinking warm ale.

I'm surprised when Captain Ryker brings me a mug. I take it gladly, and wash it down quick.

Soon we both are red-faced from drink, and our sides hurt from laughter—a rare moment for both of us.

"You need to drink more often, Commander. You are much better to be around when you're not a tight-faced bitch!" Ryker confesses humorously.

I ignore Leech's scowl. Leech has decided to remain sober.

"Lose the pair between your legs, Captain, and you will find being a female among these men isn't a simple stroll through the pines," I retort.

Ryker laughs, lifting up his mug. "Here, here!" He slaps

Leech on the back, making his scowl deepen. "What's wrong with you, Captain? A Kepper got a slice of your tongue?"

"Of course not, you drunken fool. My only concern is their guard could be surrounding us at this very moment, ready to take care of all of you, in your soon-to-be drunken slumber."

"Shit, Leech. With your sharp mind, I'm sure we'll be fine on your sober watch. Leave the Commander and me alone. For once we can stand each other's company longer than a minute."

I bob my head in agreement. "That's the truth. Here, have a drink Captain." I sweep out my mug, spilling half of it in Leech's lap. "Shit! Sorry Leech!"

Leech jumps up, takes my mug, and throws the remaining ale in the fire.

"Hey!" I shout.

"I am calling it a night, Commander. And maybe you should too."

He observes me with the gaze of a stranger, and I'm sure he has some kind of opinion of me in this state. But if he does, he keeps it to himself as he turns and leaves.

For once I don't care. I allow myself to embrace this new feeling of freedom, and disregard Leech's suggestion. I'm tired of the tension of my newfound responsibility, and the confusion of my dreams.

A few mugs of ale later, I can barely stand. The next thing I know, everything is fuzzy and someone is guiding me away from the warmth of the fire. I struggle to keep my balance, trying to find my bearings.

"Where'em going?" I slur to no one in particular. I'm still unsure who is dragging me away.

"I'm putting you to bed, Commander."

I recognize the voice as Ryker's, and somewhere deep inside I know my brain is sending signals telling me something isn't right. It's like some sort of out-of-body experience.

My legs don't do what I tell them to. Neither do my hands. Or my fingers.

Though my vision wavers, I know when we enter my tent. Ryker leads me to my bedroll, and releases me. I stumble over and fall on my back. Then his weight crashes down on top of me, his breath reeking of ale. He forces his tongue inside my mouth. I attempt to push him away.

"Gerr off me!" I yell roughly. I try to concentrate, and a flash of panic rushes over me.

Ryker sees the shift of fear rising, and he smiles deviously.

"Just hold still, Commander. It'll be over before you know it."

His hand fumbles down his trousers, and I desperately try to bring my gift to surface. I have to stop him. When I feel the familiar thrum of my gift, I smile in triumph, but when I go to use it, nothing happens.

"Having trouble?" He pulls out the bluish red stone that Bruce had with him earlier.

My breathing turns from quiet and regular to a panting gasp knowing my gift is now blocked. The air becomes thick as I bring forth all the strength I can muster to get out from under the captain.

I gasp when his cold hand finds its way down inside of my uniform. I hold back the bile that has formed in the back of my throat. His lips crush against mine and I bite his bottom lip hard. Ryker screams out angrily, and slaps me across the face, while his other hand continues to fondle me.

"Stupid bitch! Now I'm really going to let you have it. I can only imagine what the king does to you when you piss him off. It's still amazes me what he can get you to do. Even convincing you to bring an assassin force over to your home kingdom, just to bring back your own flesh and blood. Maybe he will let us men share your sister, at least."

Internally I scream; I'm not quite grasping what he's saying

—I'm just trying to find a way out of his grasp. I hate myself for not being able to control this situation. I should never have trusted myself to drink with a man who has always despised me.

He pulls my pants down and I feel the exposure of the chill air. "I, for one, will go ahead and take my payment while your body is still warm."

As he's about to enter inside me, the flap of the tent bursts open, and I hear a sword drawn. The weight of Ryker abruptly leaves me, and he cries out in pain. In moments the tent goes still.

I squint against a sudden glow inside the tent. The face holding up a lantern is none other than Nate. Looking down at my predicament, he quickly covers me up.

"Thank you." I choke as tears betray me. Karl and Murrow stumble in behind him. They take one glance at Ryker's lifeless body, then turn their attention to me.

"Is she okay, Nate?" Karl asks.

"She's fine. How is everything outside?"

"He's dead," Murrow answers.

Confusion sweeps over me. Who is dead? I push back the sharp pain that's trying to take shape behind my eyes. "What are you guys talking about?"

"We saw Ryker dragging you into your tent. Nothing looked good about it. When Kah followed to stand guard outside, we knew something was definitely wrong. So we came and checked it out. It seems we made it just in time." Nate looks tired, his eyes ringed with hollows that suggest he hasn't slept in a few days. Somehow, these touches of exhaustion only make him better looking. In fact, all of them looked exhausted. How much have they been watching over me and how have I not noticed before?

I quickly pull up my pants, and they all look away, allowing me to have a moment. When I look over and see Ryker exposed and dead, the bile can no longer stay inside. I rush out of the tent, and heave up everything from the evening.

Another lifeless body lies not too far away—Kah. Again, my stomach lurches, and it doesn't stop until there is an empty pit inside my gut. I'm thankful for the freezing temperature, as it chills the sweat that beads on my brow.

When I'm through, I go back inside, walk over to Ryker's body, and pull off the stone necklace.

"What is that?" Karl asks curiously.

I smile, a brittle smile that costs some effort. "My vulnerability. It's a stone like Bruce's."

I place the stone in my hand, and immediately drop it. "Shit! It's hot!" Picking it back up by the chain, I study it closely. There is nothing unique about it; it's just a dull-colored stone.

"What are you going to do with it?" Murrow asks.

I give it to Nate. "You take it. Keep it away from anyone who might use it against me." I stumble back down to my bedroll, a wave of exhaustion sweeping over me. Nate grabs my arm to keep me stable.

"Get some rest, Vera. Me and the guys will take care of the bodies."

I jerk back up. "No tradition!"

I explain to them what I want done with the bodies, and tell them to fetch Leech after I've slept a few hours. There are questions I need answered. Especially that clouded mention of my own flesh and blood.

IT'S JUST past midnight when Leech is brought to my tent. I'm standing, arms crossed, my face grim. Leech pauses as he looks to my friends, then back to me.

"What's going on?"

"Who sits on the throne in the West?"

"Regent Grif."

"Who's the true heir to the throne?"

"I don't know what this is about Comman—"

"I want answers, Captain. I want the truth."

Not satisfied with my reasons, he remains mute and unwilling.

"Fine," I say. "Let me tell you a story."

I fill him in on the events that unfolded after he left me alone with Ryker. He reacts exactly as I thought he would.

"That son of a bitch! I knew he was a stupid man, but I never though him capable of following through with those fantastical thoughts of his. Shit!" Then his eyes really look into mine, and I clearly see the regret in his expression. "Are you okay, Commander?"

I swallow down the disgust that I can still feel all over my body.

"Who is the heir to the throne, Captain?"

His shoulders collapse, defeated. "Your sister."

I keep from showing the hundreds of emotions that blow straight through me.

"Explain."

"King Kgar has one mission. To rule all four kingdoms. When he heard the prophecy, he knew he had to have one of the heirs, and use the heir's magic to take everything for himself. When he found out that the Western King had fathered identical twin sisters, a covert mission was put into place. However, as you know, only you were taken. Your sister was taken into hiding, and only now has been brought back to take up her kingdom."

"So it's her kingdom?" I continue to bite back the boiling heat rising under my skin.

"Yes. The reason no one came for you was because they knew she was still alive. They didn't want to sacrifice any more of their men for you. In fact, rumor has it that your sister feels threatened that you will come to usurp her throne.

She knows you are coming, and she plans to kill you on sight."

"A message for Commander Vera!"

My eyes stay on Leech. "Enter!"

A guard enters, breathing heavily. His attire is not of our uniform but of bright colors.

"Speak."

"I've just came from inside Pynth walls. I was one of the assassins on King Kgar's covert mission."

"Is Bellek with you?" I ask hopefully.

"He was captured two days ago."

I rub my forehead with firm pressure. What else would I uncover this day? A sister and the capture of Bellek, all in a day? If the girl in the golden mirror is truly my sister, she has failed to mention this tidbit of information. Maybe Leech is right; maybe she only appears to care so I will fall into her trap. She has another thing coming if she thinks I'm that easy to manipulate.

"Anything else?" I ask.

"Yes, Commander. I know the whole layout of the city and castle."

Finally, something good.

"Tell me everything."

21
_____

LIVIA

EARLY IN THE MORNING, before the sun thinks of waking, I sneak inside the training room. Right away I begin to go over what Cam taught me last evening. The footwork comes easy; the balancing reminds me of those times I walked the pine branches back home. I was nimble in the way I moved from tree to tree, and prided myself in how I never fell.

"Well, look who has the dedication of a soldier," Cam says as he approaches. I look around and see that other guards are training as well. I was so focused I didn't see them come in. "How about we throw in some foot and hand combinations?" he adds.

For the next hour Cam swings two sticks at me. I keep my eyes on the moving targets, thinking fast as I move and block the painful blows. Unfortunately I'm not always fast enough, and my shins are getting sore.

"Come on, princess. Focus. The enemy won't be this slow, or give you second chances to find your footing. You have to be diligent."

"I'm trying!" I snap. "It's not like I'll be ready in time anyway." I do my best to hold back the throbbing pain in my legs. I swear if he hits me one more time in the shin, I will take both his sticks and whack him across his throat.

"Well, you need to get close enough!" he snaps back. "If you get captured and taken to the Eastern King, there is no coming back."

I don't know if it's the frustration I'm having with his relentless training, or the reality of his words striking a nerve. Tears begin running down my face.

"Princess?" Cam asks alarmingly.

"I'm fine, I'm fine. I just feel the pressure of it all." I wipe my face. "Continue."

Cam's brow rises in question, but when he sees my face set in determination, he begins swinging his sticks. I push my frustration aside and find my calm as I do with my bow. My tension slowly melts away.

An hour goes by without us breaking; it's as if we are stuck in a trance. Sweat beads across Cam's forehead. "Fantastic!" he proclaims proudly. "That's what I'm talking about!"

Cam lowers his sticks and we both find our breath.

"We'll call this good for now. Next time we'll throw in swords." Cam smiles, and I flush with accomplishment.

"Can I ask you something?"

"Yes, Princess?"

"What do the guards think of me? Do they think I'll fail as their ruler?"

He gives me a pointed look.

"The Violet Guard has been waiting a long time for you. We've all been trained to be your protection. Your parents were the greatest leaders of them all and we all knew their heir could not be any different. So don't think for a moment, princess, that we would ever disregard your leadership or turn our backs on you. We are yours."

"Where is your place in this war?" I ask curiously.

"Next to you. Reddik informed me last night."

I push back the feeling of disappointment of not having Reddik instead. "I am honored to have you at my side."

"The honor is mine, princess." Cam bows his head slightly. "May I ask you something, princess?"

"Of course."

"What are your plans if we capture your sister?"

My eyes scan over his face, searching for the emotion behind the question.

"Welcome her home. What else would you have me do?"

"Even though she killed our men at The Wall? My brother was one of the guards killed." A flicker of anger shoots across his face.

My heart drops down to my stomach. How is it that I can find compassion for our people, but the people lack compassion for Vera? She is one of us.

I press my lips together and take a deep breath. "I'm terribly sorry for your loss, Cam. I truly am. It is a delicate situation, and I will seek the advice of Regent Grif on. Just know that she, too, is the heir of a great king and queen, and her people abandoned her. She is acting the only way she sees fit. It's still no excuse to kill so many. It's the tragedy of war, unfortunately."

Cam stares at his feet, and doesn't respond.

"Cam?" He looks up. "I truly am sorry for your loss."

"Thank you, princess."

A FEMALE RULER OF A KINGDOM: one who inherits the position by right of birth—a queen. By mere minutes, I inherited a kingdom before Vera. It could've so easily been hers. Where would Vera be now if she had been born first?

I knock on the door of the Regent's study, and wait patiently. Two Violet Guards stand by the door—one on either side-marking a subtle change of protection for my uncle. Since the intrusion, I've noticed more guards roaming the castle grounds. It gives me pause, bringing Amah's absence to the front of my mind. I believed at that moment we arrived, I would have trouble getting her to ever leave my side. Now, it seems, I barely see her.

The study door opens slightly before opening all the way. My uncle stands there in his dark grey uniform, and as always he looks the part of the Regent.

"Uncle."

"Livia...please, come in."

I follow in after him and shut the door firmly behind me.

"I'm glad you came by, there are some things we need to discuss."

"Is there something wrong?"

"No, no. Nothing like that. I want to discuss the timing of your coronation. I was hoping it would happen before war came, but it appears the enemy is much closer than I would like. Which raises the question, what do we do with you until you can become queen? We can't afford to lose you. If you do not become queen, the Western Kingdom is lost forever; there would be no hope of magic ever returning."

"What about Vera. Doesn't she have the same blood as me?" I challenge him.

"She does…"

"Then why does everyone seem to so easily forget about her? I'm not the only hope for this kingdom. Why do our people not care an inkling for her? I'm doing everything I can to learn what I need to know for the benefit of my people, and I've every intention of being their ruler. I'll rise to the occasion. But can we ignore that our own kingdom's flesh and blood was wrongfully taken away and forced to become a killer? Why didn't you go after her?"

I slump down in a chair in front of him, finally reaching the dark point of my frustration. No matter how many times I've tried to relax and work it out, it keeps coming back. I never had to worry like this in the Black Pines. I would spend days imagining this peaceful world, trying to envision a place where magic thrived and everyone lived in harmony.

I've barely been here for a week, and I've almost been kidnapped, and I've seen people die. And now I'm defending a sister I never knew I had.

"I was ordered not to, Livia," Regent Grif says. "The people were vulnerable when the raid took place. No one knew what had become of you two. When Amah sent word that she had you, it was around the same time we heard Vera was in the East. Your kingdom was ready to go and fight for her. But when I came here to pick up my sister's broken kingdom, I discouraged them."

"You are from the North. Couldn't your father have joined our forces and gone and retrieved her? That's all I ever read about in our world's history. How the two kingdoms would push back the East, keeping them behind The Wall. You outnumber them."

"My father would not risk deaths of his people. I'm sorry I have to confess this to you."

"It isn't Vera's fault. She should not be punished."

"What makes you think she would be?"

I told him of my conversation with Cam.

"It's normal for him to think that way while grieving. But she is a true heir, and she deserves to have a chance to explain. A chance to have us to listen to her, to see if she can be brought into our kingdom as one of us and not one of them. But you will find, as queen, some decisions are very difficult. We can hope that you won't need to make harsh judgment calls anytime soon."

"How do you feel, knowing she is so close?"

His dark eyes dim. "Excited, nervous—afraid. I've always wanted to see the both of you. But with Vera, I'm nervous knowing the abuse she has had to endure over the years. And because of that, I'm afraid. Afraid she will hate me for abandoning her these past sixteen years. I wish she knew the lengths I went to, the arguments I had with my father to have him support me in bringing her back. I hope she hates her king, and is being forced to come here to do his bidding."

His eyes glisten, and his voice cracks with emotion. I can see now the battle that has lived inside him. Just to know there's someone else who doesn't think her evil, helps.

"To be close to her," he continues, "and not have her here, is hard. I wish she knew the love we have for her, and how much your parents also loved her." He leans back in his chair. "The king is serious about capturing you. It makes me wonder how much Vera knows about his plan."

"What plan?"

"To have the magic of both of you. I believe he thinks if he as both magics, he can finally lash out at the Northern and Western Kingdoms. But we can't have that. Whatever deal he has made with the Enchanter can only mean destruction for us."

"Can we not negotiate? Reddik said something about the prisoner being the king's uncle. Can we not use him?"

Regent Grif shakes his head. "The king couldn't care less that we have his uncle. This is a king who murdered both of his parents. Negotiations are beneath him. But Commander Barrett knows the game of these assassins. He has trained our men diligently to be prepared for our enemy's forces."

"So what will we do with the prisoner if we can't use him to our advantage?"

"Bellek is the man who raised your sister. I hope we can use him for an advantage with Vera."

"So we basically have the person most important to her inside our castle?" Panic washes over me. Having him here could completely destroy my chance to have the kind of relationship I want with her. What will she think when she finds out he is here? "We must keep him isolated, but no harm is to come to him. If we are to have any chance to mend things with Vera, it will have to begin with trust. Bellek is that chance for trust."

Maybe I can speak with him, convince him that Vera needs to remain here in her true home. I know my uncle would not like the idea of me going down into the dungeons to speak with a prisoner. I'll have to venture there on my own.

I leave my uncle and go back to my chambers. I stand on my balcony, and look over our snow-covered city. Winter has finally come. I know it's bad timing, given that in just days a massacre will take place just beyond our walls.

The sky is washed grey, and the cold is brittle. I hope the people of Pynth do not let the weather's mood cling to them. They need to remain positive and have hope that no one will be lost. Even though I know otherwise.

"My Lady, you have company."

"Thanks, Mary. I'll be right there."

My uncle has given me a chambermaid to help with anything I might need. She is a lovely girl, eager to please. At first it was horrifying to have someone wait on me. But I quickly discovered how helpful she truly was.

I follow after her to discover Reddik standing next to our hearth. A smile comes to my lips.

"What brings you to this side of the castle?"

He waits until Mary leaves the room.

"I would like to show you something."

A glimmer shines in his eyes, and I tilt my head slightly.

"Okay?"

He holds out an arm, which I gladly take. It seems the more we find ourselves together, the more comfortable we become. He's more than just handsome; his courage in keeping me from harm and his willingness to throw his body in front of mine cannot go unremarked. He's the bravest man I know.

"So where are you taking me?"

"Patience, princess. It's a surprise." He gives me a boyish grin, and I laugh.

My whole life I've been kept away from the opposite sex, only viewing them from afar. There were times that from afar I witnessed new relationships blooming. How a man would walk up to a woman he didn't know and ask to buy her a drink. The woman's face would always turn red. But more often than not, she would leave arm in arm with the gentleman. After that, of course, I never knew what happened. But what Reddik and I have is nothing like that. This is different. And I like it.

From the moment I laid eyes on Reddik, I knew there was something about him. And the more we are around one another, the more I hope he feels the same way.

"Here we are."

I find us standing in front of a door that blends perfectly with the wall of which it is a part. If he hadn't stopped me, I would never have noticed it. He opens the door, and motions me to enter first.

The room is small and dark, except for a dim glow coming down a spiral staircase cast from antique brass. The staircase is haunting in its magical way.

Reddik closes the door behind him, and his arm brushes mine as he squeezes by. My heart pounds.

"These stairs," he says, "have been climbed many times by one single person. Not very many people know of this place, and I ask that you keep knowledge of it locked away inside yourself." A smile plays on his lips. He holds out his hand, and I take it. Who is this man, so full of mystery and surprises?

I look up as we ascend the stairs, and see them continuing to spiral to a great height. Small glassless windows dot the stone tower walls randomly, giving off a soft light. By the time we reach the top, a sheen of sweat covers both our faces.

"I know a break would've been nice, princess. But I'm too excited to show you what's behind this door."

He points to a door made of white oak, the top angling to a point. Handmade carving covers its surface, a full depiction of vines and flowers. It is beautiful.

"You go first, princess."

I reach for the antique brass handle, and the door creaks as I push it out. A cold wind whooshes around, chilling my face. I squint against the sudden brightness, and my breath catches.

We are at the top of what seems to be the tallest tower of the castle. It's covered by a domed-shaped pane of glass, and it holds an enchanting garden. Flowers of all colors have been planted in well chosen spots within a patch of neatly trimmed grass.

A stone walkway curves past these colors, through the tall walls of a hedge maze, then to a large oak tree that springs up in the center of the garden. Its branches stretch out far, creating a magical scene of beauty.

I can't control the electric feeling that sparks through my body. "This is breathtaking!"

"I'm glad you like it, princess."

I turn to him, and for once it looks as if he's blushing.

"I absolutely love it!" I say, "It reminds me of the Black Pines, living amongst the raw nature of our kingdom. It takes me back to a simpler time. Amah once told me of the love my mother had for her gardens." My words catch in my throat.

"Princess, this *is* your mother's special garden."

I cover my mouth. A breeze grabs strands of my hair, and brushes them across my face. This was my mother's?

"Would you like to walk through and see it?" he asks.

I nod numbly.

Of all the gardens in the castle, none compare to this one. We walk along the stone steps, Reddik only a step behind me. I can't believe he's brought me to this wonderful place.

Walking through the maze of hedges, I notice a mix of the plants that I grew up around. Even the red berries from a Yerba Mate bush. Their berries are known to give you energy. Amah would appreciate seeing a plant from back home. I will have to bring her here.

To my pleasant surprise, a pond is placed near the base of the large oak tree. Small fish are making ripples as they kiss the surface.

I turn around in a full circle, soaking in the garden's true beauty. I spot a large statue tucked back behind the tree, surrounded by beautiful flowers in all shades of purple.

The statue is of a beautiful woman, her expression full of joy. One of her hands is placed on her heart, while the other is outstretched, as if to take your hand.

Reddik points to the base, where words are carved.

"My heart fills with joy, seeing them so happy." -Queen Kyra

A sadness crushes over me.

"How I wish I could've met her. Already my life has changed in so many ways, exposed to so many realities that I never imagined. It seems so long ago now that I was standing on the branch of a black pine, not having the burdens I do now."

As much as I try to hold it in, pain comes nonetheless. It begins as a feeling in my chest and a sadness in my brain, and leads to a tear sliding down my cheek.

"I ,too, never knew my mother," he says.

His confession startles me. "What? What about the funeral?"

"She was not my mother. My mother was a Lady of the Icewyn Court. She died giving birth to me."

"So Oliver isn't your brother?"

"Half-brother. My father is Lord Afton, an advisor to King Dowd of Icewyn."

"You are from the North? Like my uncle?"

He nods. "I am. I came here with your uncle when he was

instructed to by our king. I was nine at the time, and I assisted your uncle in everything. Being the son of a Lord, my training started young, and I took it upon myself to perfect it. My future relied on it."

"Why?"

"Because I, too, would one day be an advisor to a king. Like my father before me. In our kingdom, advisors are also protectors. So I was prepared and trained in many different forms of arts."

Hearing him tell me of his life shows me another layer of him that I find intriguing.

"Around eight years ago," he explains, "my father traveled to a village to help with an issue that was getting out of hand. His mission was to uproot the problem, and carry out a punishment, relieving the village of the unwanted suffering. I never understood why an advisor would be bothered with such a task, but a few years ago, I uncovered the truth." He takes a deep breath. "He had one night of pure passion with a maiden, and she was later discovered to be with child—his child. She refused to be rid of the baby, and he in turn shunned her. I was never intended to find out this secret. But I did, three years ago. I was ashamed of how my father handled it, and I traveled to this village where I met my half-brother. I promised his mother that I would take care of him if anything should befall her."

He doesn't say anymore, and he doesn't have to. I know the rest. He, too, has to hold responsibility on his shoulders that should never have been his. It's comforting to share our grief with one another. It makes the world feel less alone.

I wish both my parents were here to give me guidance. But this can never happen. I still don't know what to think of the darker side of my gift. I'm disgusted with myself for unleashing that atrocity. Blood is now on my hands, and I will never be able to wash them clean. This is a guilt that adds to the weight on my shoulders.

For once the wind is quiet, allowing me to feel a moment of peace.

"I'm sorry you never had a chance to know her," he says.

"Me, too."

"I am sorry you have to deal with this sudden role thrown upon you. If it makes any difference, I believe you have adjusted seamlessly."

"Thanks. I feel a mess, like a newborn deer stumbling to take its first steps."

"Princess, what happened to that assassin in Pynth?"

I step back, startled by his forthrightness. I look down, shame washing over me.

"I killed him with my gift. I'm ashamed. I should never have been blessed." I want to curl up in a dark hole.

"It was self-defense, princess. No one would ever fault you for it." His voice is soft and gentle. I shake my head in response, and fight the urge to cry.

"Livia."

I choke back my tears and lift my eyes to his. This is the first time he's ever addressed me by name. I feel a shift in the air and a stirring deep inside me. His hand reaches up and touches my hair, pushing it away from my face.

"Don't ever apologize," he says, "for the spark that lives inside you."

His eyes shift down to my mouth, and my heart nearly stops. He leans in and presses his lips to mine.

My world falls away.

It's a feeling I've never experienced before, yet it is everything I thought it would be—magic. When he pulls back, affection glows in his eyes, and my cheeks warm.

"You are truly a pure and honest person." He takes my hand. "It is a rare thing to see. I found myself drawn to you the moment I met you, and I've made it my own mission to protect you."

"But that isn't your duty."

"My duty is to Regent Grif. It seems, however, I've naturally gravitated to you instead," he says and laughs. "Don't tell him that."

"Never," I say with a smile, "It surprises me you feel this way. I mean, I hoped you would."

He rubs his thumb over my hand. "It surprises me, too. But you keep doing things that I can't help but admire."

"Me? Like what?" I don't feel like I've done anything of real value. What could there possibly be for him to admire?

"For starters, your determination to rescue my brother, and then heal him."

"Anyone would do that."

He shakes his head. "No, not anyone. Also, he told me what you said at the stables. Making sure he was okay."

I shake my head. These are only simple things.

"Then your dedication to the people. You spend all your free time studying everything you can find that might help them. And I'm not ignoring that you squeezed in time to practice with a sword." His face leans in again, stopping an inch from mine. "Then you saved me. I felt the heat of your magic course through me. I knew it was you."

He kisses me again. This time I kiss back fiercely, and his arms wrap around me, bringing me against his body. A tingle spreads through me, and I don't want this moment to stop.

Reddik's lips freeze against mine.

"Did you hear that?" he whispers, his breath warm on my lips.

I wait and listen. Then I hear it—the faint bang of a drum.

Reddik takes my hand and leads me to the edge of the tower, pushing back a tangle of ivy.

The sun is steadily making its way down, casting dark shadows over the land. Off in the distance, specks of shadows trickle over the horizon. The time has finally come. The Silent Watchers are here.

22

VERA

I HAVE ALWAYS HEARD whispers of the glamor of Willobourne Castle. It was built on a mountain island. However, no one has prepared me for the magnificent beauty of the entire city that lies before me. Colors pop up from behind the wall, homes appear with peaked shingled roofs, all giving only a glimpse of what lies within.

But I know already what lies inside those walls—fear. It was my idea to have the continuous bang of a drum announce our arrival.

The drum's steady beat fills the dead air of their sky. This sound will seep into their minds and lock in that fear, driving them delirious.

The ground is covered in the white snows of winter. After the heavy snowfall yesterday, the top layer is a perfect powder of white. Either we will sink down into it and plough through, or there will be a bottom to it that will be frozen enough to march over. Either way it won't last long. With the thousands of men crossing over, the snow will soon be trampled down enough that it won't matter.

I sit atop Provena, gazing over the dark, quiet city. The moon shines high in the sky, the cumulous clouds having parted, allowing me to see the Violet Guard standing at attention—matching the stillness of the night and the fortified walls that stand around the city. Nothing is moving. I'm almost impressed by their control, but it doesn't compare to the discipline and fearlessness that's always exemplified by the Silent Watchers.

The seed of fear resides in the westerners, and the moment I release these ferocious assassins, that seed will grow, and they will discover the meaning of true fear.

But I'm not ignorant. I know many of my men will die in this battle.

I might even die.

Once I am back at camp, I go sit with Nate, Murrow, and Karl near the warmth of a fire. I've decided to keep them close at all times.

When the camp woke up this morning, they discovered two men speared on two sharpened trees with a sign posted above them reading: TRAITORS.

I remember hearing the murmurs throughout the camp, and they continued on as we moved out, as more men were able to view the blue-skinned bodies with glossed-over eyes.

The message spoke loud and clear. There would be no traditional burial for them. They were to be left behind to be ravaged by the beasts of the forest. I hadn't cared to know the thoughts of my men.

A lot of the men spit on them, supporting my decision without knowing the grievance. I moved those men closer to me. I will need to be surrounded by those I know I can trust. I know Ryker had plenty of cronies, and I'm not sure which ones they are.

"I've decided to rescue Bellek. You will come with me."

"Geez, Commander, so needy," Murrow jokes.

I roll my eyes and look to Nate. He watches me closely, and I don't know why, but it makes me feel so fully aware of myself that I casually toss my braid over my shoulder.

"We will follow you wherever you want to go," he says.

"I'm counting on it. And if anything happens to me but not to you, get out. Take Zyrik and run. Run far away, and never let the king touch him ever again."

They firmly nod. I know they will do that for me without hesitation. I explain my plan.

I LIE IN MY BEDROLL, staring at the roof of my tent. The moment I settled in, the thoughts inside my head began to whirl. I've been trying to keep certain thoughts tucked away, but I know that soon enough I will face betrayal.

How long did Bellek think he could keep me from knowing about my sister? What hurts more is I always thought he wanted the best for me. But his keeping this secret makes him just part of the king's plans.

From as far back as I remember, Bellek did his best to keep me away from the king's abusive grasp. Most the time it didn't work. King Kgar didn't need an excuse to hurt me, but he always found one. Anything and everything I did was wrong and warranted punishment.

I remember when I was the same age as Zyrik, and the king discovered me in the kitchens with a smile on my face. I had just eaten a fresh piece of bread the baker gave me, and it was the best thing I'd ever had. He hit me hard with his hand, and I fell from the force of it. He watched as I choked on the morsel, and I was lucky it came up when it did. He proceeded to drag me out of the room, yelling at me.

Smiling, then almost dying, was to be all my fault. He told his uncle that if I couldn't be controlled, I would live with a chain around my neck and be shackled to his ankle.

Punishment after punishment was delivered. I don't even remember a time where I didn't have a cut or a bruise from the king. But I know it could've been worse. Bellek kept me at his side, training me up to develop that hard outer surface, the only protection he could find for me against the king.

But when I turned fourteen, Bellek could't protect me from the king's late night visits. And from the lingering touches I felt in the morning, once the king had left. I knew Bellek would kill the king if he knew. There were many times I almost shared my dark nightmares with him.

But I was afraid. What if the king should have Bellek killed? Just for knowing. I would be entirely left to the king's whims. No, I would keep my secrets for Bellek's protection. And for my own.

So why do I now feel that Bellek has slapped me in the face? He knew I could be queen of a kingdom, surrounded by thousands of guards. Why does he go along with the king when I know he doesn't agree with anything he does?

Knowing I have a sister has shaken my world. It's not that I have a relation, but that there's another person in my life who should be wanting the best for me, but instead would rather see me dead.

I allow my anger to build up. I will rely on it to get me through the outer wall and into the dungeons. My first mission is Bellek. Then it will be finding my sister and taking her to the king. And then it will be her turn to face him.

23

GOLDEN MIRROR

THE GIRLS STARE at one another. They both know the truth.

Vera: *So, you are my sister.*

Livia: *Yes. And you and the assassins are here.*

Vera: *Yes.*

Livia: *Do you plan to take me?*

Vera shows no emotion.

Vera: *I do. I also plan to take back the king's uncle.*

Livia's eyes widen.

Vera: *Did you not think I would find out about you having him?*

Livia: *I didn't know. I mean, I knew, but I didn't know if I should tell you.*

Vera: *You thought me a fool, sister? Did you think I would fall for your lies? I know you care nothing for me. I know two queens can't rule a kingdom. I would only be in your way.*

Livia: *That's not true! I want you here with me. I've never wanted you out of the way. Whoever told you that is not speaking the truth.*

Vera: *The person who told me has been more of a family to me than your entire kingdom put together. A kingdom that never once came to save me.*

Livia: *Look, I didn't even know you existed until a week ago. I didn't even know I was an heir to this kingdom. But I do know I've always longed for my true family. That is you. I need you.*

Vera: *You don't need me. But I do need you—to keep those I love alive, and to keep his hands off me. That's why I need you.*

Livia: *You would turn me over to that man? I'm offering you a safe haven. What else do you need?*

Vera: *Nothing. I need nothing else.*

Livia: *Surely there is something. Let me help you.*

Vera: *Put yourself in chains and walk out to me. That would help me.*

LIVIA TAKES her hand off the mirror, and steps back. This girl is not the sister she envisioned. Her mind is warped into thinking only lies. There is only one more thing she can try before all hope is lost.

24

LIVIA

My footsteps echo off cold, damp stone walls as I descend into the dungeon. The light from my lantern flickers in the dark. It didn't take long to find out where the wing for prisoners was located. A simple question masked with concern, and my chambermaid let it slip without guessing my intent.

I can still feel the brush of Reddik's lips on my own. The moment we discovered the Silent Watchers on the horizon, we both rushed to find Regent Grif. Luckily for us, Commander Barrett was already aware of the Watchers' location, and the Violet Guard was already in position.

Come morning, I would be in a secured location—my chambers. I remember laughing at the idea, thinking it was a joke, but I soon discovered it was anything but. Reddik explained that in the morning, the corridors that lead to my chambers will be lined with guards, all at the ready to protect me from harm.

I don't know why, but I feel that I am turning my back on my own men. They'll need me with them to use my gift. I tried to explain all this, but no one will listen. *For you to be out there is out of the question.* But any of them dying will place a considerable amount of guilt on my shoulders, when I could save them.

I slept for only a few hours, waking up in despair. Vera wasn't budging. I could not convince her of my help. That's when I knew I had to visit Bellek.

I finally reach the dungeon door. It takes most of my strength to pry it open. Soon I have it scraping across the stone floor, giving me enough room to slip inside.

Spooky doesn't quite cover what I feel, and eerie is an understatement. A chill creeps over me, seeing dark shadows cast across what feels like a large open space. A dim light glows up high, displaying a single chain hanging down in the center of the room.

The moment I take a step towards it, the entire room lights up. An unseen flame reflects off the white domed ceiling above. The light that had spotlighted the chain is now gone, and it now hangs from a mouth of darkness.

"Welcome."

I turn quickly at the sound of a man's voice. He's a tall man, made of nothing but bones in the shape of a body. He has short-cropped hair, and translucent skin that seems never to have seen the light. I shudder.

He crosses the room, keys jingling at his side. He stops when he reaches the center of the room, where the chain hangs above his head. He clasps his hands in front of him.

"And who are you?"

"I'm Princess Livia," I answer hesitantly. "W…who are you?"

"I am Les. The key holder. I wasn't expecting such an important visitor. Come, tell me of your love for making music."

"Excuse me? I don't know what you mean." I scratch nervously at my arm. "I'm here to see a prisoner by the name of Bellek. If you will take me to him, I'll be on my way."

"He's quite the popular one these days. But I cannot take you to him."

"Why not?"

"He just had a visitor. Too much music," he explains, "and it will make chaos with the others."

I don't understand his mention of music. But I have no desire to ask, afraid of what he might say.

"Who was this visitor?"

Les shakes his head. "Secrets, secrets, you won't see. Secrets, secrets, safe with me."

A laugh bubbles out from his throat; he seems thrilled with his own rhyme. Tired of this game, I notice a barred door behind him. I cross the room quickly, and grab the handle.

"Stop!" he shouts.

He rushes over and swipes my hand aside. "You cannot enter!"

"Let her through, Les."

I whip around to find Amah standing behind us.

"Amah! What are you doing here?"

"I would ask you the same, En Oli."

"I've come to speak with Bellek."

Her sharp gaze pierces me. "Les, hand her the key."

"Yes, my lady," he says.

I look between the two, confused. Do they know one another? Les takes a key off the ring at his waist, and hands it to me, showing me all his teeth as he does so. Of which I am surprised he has any.

"Now you can go play music with Amah. She is the best at making the beautiful sounds," he says.

"That's enough, Les," Amah interrupts, "I'll take it from here."

Les nods, crosses the room, and disappears behind another door.

"Who is that man?" I ask Amah curiously.

"He is a man who started here as a boy. His father did this

before him, and he followed in his father's footsteps. He might seem strange, but he's brilliant, and I wouldn't try putting anything past him. So, you are here on your own?"

"Yes. I didn't think anyone would care to join me."

"You have no business down in these parts. But I have a feeling there'll be no convincing you of that. Are you sure you are prepared for what you might see?"

I try to swallow past the lump in my throat. I nod.

"Then let's get on with it," she says.

Amah reaches past me and pulls open the door. I notice scrapes on her knuckles and I'm about to ask her about them, when something inside me tells me not to.

"I haven't seen much of you lately," I say instead.

"No?" she replies, "It seems, maybe, you are doing fine without me."

"I would never say that. You know that."

She looks back and nods. "Yes, I know that."

Light trickles down the corridor as a sickly green glow. We pass door after door, walking along damp floors. It's strange to think an entire ocean is beyond these walls. A single crack would be devastating.

"Amah? What did Les mean by making music?"

Amah doesn't respond. We have reached the end of the hall. She peeks through a small window, then steps back and motions for me to look inside. I see a bulky form sitting against the back wall, his arms dangling from chains high above him. It's Bellek.

I push open the heavy door, and the pungent smell of filth greets me. I step closer to the prisoner, and light from the hall is cast over him. I barely recognize him.

A gash runs down the side of this man's face, and both of his eyes are swollen shut. His once clean-shaven head is now covered in crusted blood, which also covers the bright clothes he wears. He looks nothing like the man I saw in the streets of Pynth.

My body locks up with an unknown rage. "What happened to this man?" I ask sharply. It takes everything for me not to yell. "I said no harm should be done to him." I look to Amah. "Who did this?"

The cell remains silent, Amah's eyes look defiantly into mine.

Bellek violently coughs, and I turn back to him.

"Vera?" He speaks hoarsely.

He coughs again, then slumps forward, dangling from his chains. I go and place my hands on either side of his face, and close my eyes. I push my gift through him, taking note of all the fractured bones in his face. I quickly mend them, and calm the swelling.

His head comes back up, and he slowly opens his eyes.

"Vera?" he asks again.

"I am her sister," I reply, "Livia."

He tries to wet his chapped lips. It pains me to see him like this. What Vera would think if she saw him right now.

Suddenly he jerks forward, knocking me down to the ground. Amah rushes forward and kicks him hard in the side. Bellek cries out in pain.

I scramble up, and quickly wipe the sludge from my hands. I grab Amah's arm and push her back.

"Stop it! Don't lay another hand on him, you hear me? I will not stand for this. What has become of you?"

"He is the enemy, Livia."

"So is Vera! Are you going to kick her, too?"

"Of course not!" Amah snaps.

"Don't trust a single word that comes out of that crazy torturous bitch's mouth," Bellek shouts unexpectedly.

"So it was you?" I say. "You did this to him?"

"It was I."

I take a step back, shaking my head. "Why?" Time and time again, Amah keeps proving to me that I really don't know her.

"Before there was you, there was your father," she explains. "And before your father, there was Queen Myrtle—your grandmother. She plucked me out from the Temple, and trained me to be an assassin. Your father's assassin. It's all I know. Raising you forced me to keep all that locked away. I became soft, as I had to. I had to raise a future queen. You were and still are my life. You are all that remains of your father, a man I loved." She points to Bellek. "This man would try to take you from me. I will not see that done—ever."

"I don't even know who you are anymore," I say. "From the moment I turned sixteen, I have been told so many hidden truths. I've had to discover who I am, and with no help from you." My anger releases, "You had sixteen years to tell me these things! This whole time I was living with you, I was living with the very thing that was hunting me—an assassin. What makes you any better than them? I can't have you here in this cell with me. I need to convince this man to reach Vera for me. I can't have you in my way, ruining that. Leave."

"En Oli…"

"Leave! Before I say something I might regret!"

Pain flickers across her face, then she turns and leaves.

I push my anger aside. I can't waste any more time. Now I must convince this broken man that I'm the good guy—I sigh and try to collect my calm.

I place my hands back on Bellek, and begin the healing process again. But before I get too far in, I'm jarred back to reality and find myself sprawled out on my back. I get back up, and I see his nostrils flare.

"I don't need your healing touch. I wear my scars proudly, and I don't need you taking them away."

"I was only trying to help."

"Help?" The corners of his mouth turn down. "Why would you do such a thing?"

"It's the right thing to do."

His eyes turn into thin slits. "I don't believe you."

"Well, you should. You should also believe me when I say, Vera is right outside these walls, and my mission is to keep her here—where she'll be safe. I need you to help me accomplish that."

"I will not."

"Does Vera not mean anything to you, then? You mean everything to her."

"How do you know this?"

"I just know. You and your assassins are her family. But King Kgar, what is he to her? A tyrant? A monster? How long must you watch her suffer under your nephew's rule? I know she will come and rescue you. And I will let her. But you must convince her to stay. Where she'll be safe."

Bellek drops his head once more, and I fear he's passed out.

"Get out and leave me be," he whispers roughly.

"Will you do as I sug—"

"I said, get out!"

I shut my mouth. I knew he wouldn't be easily convinced. But I've planted the seed and that's all I can do for now. I leave his cell, locking the door securely behind me. Now I must wait, and pray to the Maker my plan works.

25

VERA

THE VIOLET GUARD waits for our movement with thousands of arrows, all with sharpened points, ready to be unleashed. Silent Watchers stand in formation behind me, the bright sky illuminating their red masks. Today's the day blood will be shed.

Silence fills the horizon where thousands of assassins transform the silence to fear. I attempt to grab the minds of the enemy's archers across the distance that separates us, but it's too far. Bringing my fist up in the air, I signal thousands of shields up, a crisp coordinated motion creating a sound that echoes off into the distance. With a slight rotation of my fist, we move.

We move as one, a sea of red and black, as if we are one mind instead of many. Right legs move in unison, and then left legs. With each step the sound of boots on the frozen ground is like the warning thunder of a coming storm. Their masks block the frigid wind from the grim faces I know are behind them.

I grab hold of my Warriors Necklace, and kiss the grey stones for encouragement. After I talked with my sister, I realized how important this mission will be. Bringing her to

Kgar could very well give me the chance to escape with Zyrik and leave the king's crudeness far behind. If he's going to war for her, then her gift is obviously stronger than mine.

As I predicted, a rain of arrows showers over us. I hear their thuds as they bounce off assassin shields. I've brought mine up in time to catch the force of arrow after arrow.

"Ladders!" I yell. "Catapults!

The assassins part, revealing large barbaric siege weapons. It takes many assassins to push them forward.

The scaling ladders run ahead of us and Violet Guards take aim. Arrows pierce assassins, but others readily take their place, and our force continues strong.

My gift rumbles beneath my skin, eager to be unleashed. As we march closer, I feel my mind beginning to lock onto theirs. Not wasting a single second, I latch onto those heartbeats that wear the silver tree emblem, and crush them.

Hundreds of men drop like flies, dead before they hit the ground. I center my energy quickly when more archers take their place, and I lash out again. This time, it's the sound of bones cracking that fills the cold silent air.

"Release!"

Massive stones soar through the air and shake their walls. The catapults creak under the pressure, and assassins quickly place the next stones. There's still more to be done.

The battering ram is assembled, and I send it to the gate. I prevent the Violet Guard from taking the men down. This moment is the test of my reborn magic. It has yet to waver against my continuous use. They hit strong, then retrace their steps to repeat.

"Release the Keppers!"

Captain Leech whistles a high-pitched tone, and the ferocious birds of prey echo back in a matching pitch. Soon, Keppers are casting shadows over us as they fly over and sweep through those archers yet out of my range. The

Kepper's talons are outstretched, inflicting damage. Painful cries confirm they've hit their mark.

Men rush up the ladders and battle ensues atop the wall. It's only a matter of time before it continues on down the other side.

"Commander, look!"

Nate points to a large crack in the wooden gate. We wait in anticipation, until under pressure the gate gives way. Their guards are ready on the other side, slicing through our men. I push them back with my gift and let my men tear down the rest of the gate.

Thousands of Silent Watchers pour into the city. I maneuver Provena through them, casting my gift out, blinding their guards. My men cut them down quickly, and move on. I finally get ahead of my men and the sound of Provena's hooves hitting the cobblestones is like hammers on an anvil. My friends follow close behind me.

Violet Guards are everywhere; I keep my mind in constant motion to hold them off. We hurry past them, and are long gone before my gift releases them.

More soldiers await us at the bridge's gate. I reach down inside myself again and grab hold of my gift. But something's wrong with my store of energy. The amount I used earlier must have depleted me.

"I don't know how many I can hold," I yell. "We'll have to fight our way through!"

We draw our swords and prepare to face their men. Arrows fly through the air, and our shields come up.

I try again to ignite my gift, and it faintly comes back to surface, enough to snap the archer's arms. The rest of them charge, swords drawn, unafraid of us—just four riders coming their way.

Our horses knock them to the ground. I swing my sword, steel meeting steel, trying to clear a path to the gate. A loud shriek shoots through the sky, announcing a Kepper. Their men shout, and duck for cover. Not all of the men are lucky, as the large, sleek bird dives towards the ground, scooping one up. He screams in pain as sharp black talon pierces his body.

The Kepper throws the dead remains aside and swoops again. The beastly bird's talons extend out, and slice through a line of men, whose sinew and flesh gives way. Inner contents splatter to the ground, staining the white snow beneath.

"Watch it, Vera!" Murrow throws a knife, and it whizzes past me, sticking into the throat of a Violet Guard behind me. Murrow gives me a curt nod, before turning to attack another soldier. Finally, my gift comes roaring back in full force, and I demolish the rest.

"Oh, come on!" Karl shouts. "I almost had him!" He looks down at his opponent, now dead.

"We don't have time to play around," I say. "Let's get in and get out."

We race across the bridge towards the ornate architecture of the white palace that towers ahead of us. To think, this is where I once longed to live. I swallow the bitter taste of regret.

I look back over my shoulder and see a mass of Silent Watchers coming up behind us. I smile. This is our time.

I PULL on Provena's reins, stopping us inches from the edge where the drawbridge is raised. I try to peer under my shield as arrows rain down on us. I grab hold of enemies I see and cast them aside. I spot a man in the tower next to the gate. I reach inside his mind to make him take his sword and begin to cut away the chain holding up the bridge. It takes time and I control a few other men to help him. Finally, I manage to orchestrate success.

The last chain is cut and the bridge comes crashing down. I face my assassins. "Bring the battering ram. Now!"

Minutes go by before the assassins begin running the ram into the last gate. I continue blocking the Violet Guard until all of them place their focus on me. I hide underneath my shield, along with some assassins who place theirs up with mine. The arrows never cease, continuing on in a steady rhythm, some even puncturing partly through.

We have to be almost through the gate. Why is it taking so long? I begin counting massive hits, until I hear the crunch of the gate breaking away.

We rush through, and soon enough we've infiltrated the castle. My small group breaks away, hurrying towards the dungeon.

I was told where the winding staircase would be, and we follow it down. Nate pulls back a heavy door, and we rush into a large, circular, domed room. There's a soft glow of light circling above us, and I notice a single chain hanging from its center.

"There are too many doors in here," Karl says. "Which one is it?"

"It's that one." I point across the room to a barred door. Rushing over, I yank on it, but it doesn't budge.

"You'll need a key to get inside."

A scrawny man in long grey robes appears behind us, a large ring of keys hanging at his waist. I immobilize him and take them.

"Thanks for letting us know," I sneer.

I throw them at Murrow, who catches them and immediately starts on the lock. He tries the keys one by one until one catches. It's amazing how things are going my way.

I suddenly fall to the ground, clasping my hands over my ears. The sound of a thousand cries roars inside my head. I look over to the strange man, and he's pulling on the chain in the center of the room. Whatever he's just done, I know we're screwed. In my overconfidence, I released him, not knowing what he could do.

His strange half-smile infuriates me, and I burst his heart inside his chest. He crumbles to the floor to become a heaping pile of rags. The release of the chain silences the bell.

"Hurry, let's go!" I scream.

The bell ringing is still echoing in my head as we run down a long narrow corridor. We pause at every door to look inside, and it isn't long before I hear Nate yell from up ahead. "He's here!"

Murrow tries the keys again until we hear the familiar click. I push open the door.

"It's about time," Bellek says, as he steps out from the shadows.

Bruises lie fresh on his face and down his neck into the simple robes he wears. I watch his eyes shift to my necklace and his grim expression falters.

"We need to hurry,' I say, "before we get trapped down here."

Bellek steps forward. "Vera."

"Don't," I interrupt. "I came here planning to yell at you. But we don't have time. You'll have to wait to receive my wrath." I pin him with a frosty glare and his mouth sets into a hard line.

We run swiftly through the damp hall and into the circular chamber where we sidestep the limp body; we bound up the stairs and into the main hall.

A hundred men with drawn swords greet us. From the corner of my eye I see an archer release an arrow. My eyes widen as I watch the arrow pierce Bellek's chest. He stumbles back and drops to the floor.

In that moment, my vision turns violet, and the hairs on my arm stand on end. The Violet Guards aren't prepared for my reaction. I cast out my hands, and scream, crushing their bones. These bastards will never be my family.

26

LIVIA

I WRING my hands watching the battle unfold in the distance. I can only imagine the damage being inflicted, and I'm afraid to find out once the dust clears what will be left. I just found my true home, and it's crumbling before me.

Moments ago I watched Vera and her men battle across the bridge; I pray she finds Bellek. I gave orders for his cell to be cleaned, and him as well of his own stink. He still wouldn't let me completely heal him, but I convinced him a bath wouldn't hurt.

"Livia, you must find your calm," my uncle presses. "Even if they get through, their orders are not to harm you. You'll be fine."

Fine? What about them. I take a deep breath. I hope he knows I care for his well-being, too.

I glance behind me. Reddik's leaning against the mantel talking intently to Cam. They have kept plenty to themselves, going over who knows what. Each time Reddik catches me staring, a flutter thrills inside me.

Since visiting my mother's garden we haven't had a second to ourselves. His duty is to Regent Grif, but I can tell he's worried about me as well.

"What in the Maker's name?" I return my attention to Regent Grif. I follow his gaze and see two large red birds in the sky.

"What are they?" I ask, alarmed.

"Keppers," Amah answers. She steps out from the curtain's shadow, where she has been keeping her silence. "They are said to be vicious creatures."

"Well, these vicious creatures are coming right for us!" I observe, my panic rising.

Reddik rushes over to the door and opens it; he barks orders to the soldiers and they file in swiftly, their swords at the ready.

I am frozen in place watching these monstrous birds get closer, until I am knocked to the floor by Amah. Seconds later, Keppers crash through the windows, shattering glass and scattering it across the room.

Two red beasts with the blackest of eyes begin ripping our guards to shreds.

"En Oli, come!" Amah shouts. "Keep low and follow me."

Glass shards cover the floor like thousands of tiny daggers. I carefully follow Amah, staying close to the room's wall and avoiding as much glass as possible. I glance towards the chaos just as sharp talons slice through a soldier. I watch in horror as bright red blood is flung against the wall. My heart stops as Reddik approaches the Kepper. In on fluid motion his sword cuts the bird's head off; the head tumbles to Reddik's feet.

Regent Grif pushes me and Amah through the doorway, follows and quickly slams the door behind him.

"What about Reddik and Cam!" I cry.

The door flies open, and Reddik and Cam rush out, followed by three other guards. We take a moment to allow them to catch their breath. I notice flecks of blood on Reddik's face, and I'm thankful it's not his.

"We must go to another room and batten the Regent and princess in," Reddik huffs out.

"Mine is near—we can hold them there," Amah suggests.

I stay quiet as they discuss to as what to do with me; irritation bristles over me. I am right here and they act as if I'm not to have a say.

"We need to go help our people," I say. But it seems no one hears me. So I turn and face the guards who await orders. "I need an escort, who will come?"

In unison they snap to attention.

"What do you think you are doing?" Amah asks.

"Fighting back! Healing! Anything besides standing around and waiting for trouble to knock at our door. Which if you haven't noticed, already has happened. So I am taking any of you who want to come, to go help our men."

Regent Grif places his arm on mine. "Livia, you can't be exposed so."

"Then don't let them capture me. But I'm going."

I turn and leave, and everyone follows.

The first men we come across are dead. I kneel down beside one and try desperately to find a pulse—but nothing.

Cam and Reddik come running down the hall. The moment I decided to go on this venture, they had half the men run ahead to secure a clear path for me.

"You need to come take a look at this," Reddik says briskly to Regent Grif. He avoids looking at me but he can't hide his worried expression.

"Take me, too," I demand.

Reddik's lips thin and his eyes shift to mine. It is clear he doesn't want me to see what he has found. But he doesn't argue and turns back, motioning for us to keep quiet as he leads us to where he's just been.

I know from the rows of stone statues that we are on the second floor and that the corridor leads to the main hall's gallery.

Reddik signals for everyone to stop except for me and Regent Grif. We follow him through one of the many doors that lead out onto the gallery's overlook. Silence fills the space. Reddik motions for us to squat down before we go to look over the ledge. I gasp when I look out over the scene. Reddik covers my mouth and pulls me back. "They mustn't see you," he breathes. I nod that I understand, and he releases me. I edge my way back out onto the ledge.

A hundred men lie dead on the main floor—a graveyard of the unburied. All dead but for a small group of assassins—and my sister.

My veins chill. Did she kill these men? Is killing all my sister is capable of? I swallow back the bile in my throat.

The assassins shift and an uneasiness settles over me. Laying on the ground with an arrow sticking out of his chest is Bellek.

I startle when Reddik touches my arm. He motions for me and my uncle to return to the hall. The image of my sister standing among the dead churns my stomach. Unable to hold in the bile any longer, I rush to a statue along the wall. My stomach heaves until it is empty.

"What did you see?" Amah interjects.

I try to ignore Reddik's muttered explanation.

I hear a shout and look over my shoulder. Two soldiers are dragging another by the arms, rushing him to my feet.

"We found him still breathing, but only barely," one of the soldiers huffs out.

I kneel down and place my hand on the crusted blood on his head. I close my eyes and work quickly, mending the injury and returning him back to health.

A door bursts open as I open my eyes. A mass of assassins comes running through and I scramble to my feet. Their weapons are drawn, and they're led by a giant man with gruesome scars splaying out from beneath his mask.

Cam plants himself in front of me as guards draw their

swords. Amah, however, rushes pass me and screams at the top of her lungs. She sounds feral and deadly. The Violet Guards follow her, their swords meeting those of our enemies.

Reddik rushes me. "Take this." He hands me one of his short blades before dashing away to Regent Grif.

Cam has his sword up, preparing to greet those who are able to slip through our guards. "Princess, stay behind me! No matter what."

I inch back and step behind another statue. I watch as the chaos unfolds. Amah's blade meets that of the scarred man blow for blow, refusing to give him any advantage. She fights viciously, as if her life depends on it.

Regent Grif is nearby and locked in a battle of his own, with Reddik at his back and engaged with another. They both seem one with their blades as they take down their opponents with ease.

Amah falling to the ground grabs my attention. My heart pounds inside my chest seeing her scramble away from the assassin's deadly blows. Get up, Amah, get up! Amah maneuvers quickly and rolls to her side, but it isn't good enough. The assassin arcs his blade, cutting her across her abdomen.

"Nooo!!" I speed towards Amah with Cam shouting after me. But I'm too quick and I throw myself over Amah, hoping to block the assassin's killing blow. I squeeze my eyes shut as a sharp pain shoots over the side of my head. My last thought before I black out is how warm and wet my hands are from being on Amah.

27

VERA

COME ON, Bellek. Wake up. Wake up! I slap him hard across the face. He coughs roughly as he looks down at his chest. "Shit!" He rests his head back on the ground, and takes a deep breath.

"W...what do you want me to do?" I stutter.

"Use one of your knives," he says, "and cut it low."

I swallow. "Okay." I grab one of the knives at my belt and begin sawing on the shaft. He cringes and gasps. Nate, Murrow, and Karl kneel down and hold him steady.

When the shaft snaps off Nate offers his hand to help Bellek up. Surprisingly the stubborn man takes it. I look around the room to the devastation I caused. How many more will I have to kill before this war is over? I should feel guilty for my actions, but I don't. All I feel is a numbness, as if my feeling receptors have been burned away. When my sister finds how much blood is on my hands, I doubt she'll want me at her side—not now.

"Was that Bruce who ran by with all those men?" Bellek gruffs.

"Yeah. Leave it to Bruce to show up right after Vera's done the hard part," Murrow scoffs.

"He's probably looking for my sister. I knew the king wouldn't completely trust me to do the job."

Bellek clenches his jaw. "Vera, I need to tell you…" He stops at the sound of footsteps coming towards us. We quickly position ourselves around Bellek, and I keep my mind sharp.

Bruce comes bursting back down the grand staircase carrying a girl. He bounds over scattered bodies and rushes past us. The long, black hair that flows behind him tells me it's Livia.

I take off after him, maneuvering between fallen men, then out the front doors. Bruce begins strapping Livia to his horse, and I rush to Provena and prepare to follow.

Bellek and the others find horses of their own and we take after Bruce across the bridge. We ride swiftly through the city, our horses hurdling fallen soldiers from both sides, and bypassing bursts of battles along the way, my gift keeping our path clear.

A large section of the outer wall lies in shambles. Bodies are scattered over the ground; dust still rises from the debris. We gallop through the fallen gate, and enter into the clangor of sword fighting. The once perfect white snow across the covered field is now a bloodied slush, littered with hundreds of lifeless bodies. In between battlements and under our shifting feet, I see stray limbs and more corpses—once men, who are no longer recognizable. Red masks lay strewn around—more than I can count.

The moment we reach camp, Captain Leech comes out to greet us. "Commander Vera! Bellek! Am I ever glad to see you both alive."

"Captain," I say.

"How are our men doing on the inside?" he asks.

"Still fighting strong. Unfortunately, too many of our own are being cut down."

He nods grimly.

"Our healer is set up inside the tent," he says to Bellek. "It seems you might need to visit."

"Mind your business," Bellek grumbles.

I look over my shoulder and see Bruce grabbing supplies and latching them to his saddle. He isn't wasting any time getting the king's prize to him. I know I have to follow.

"Bellek, I have to go with Bruce. I reinstate you as Commander of the Silent Watchers. They're all yours now."

"Hold your horse, Vera. I need a moment."

He leads me away from the others. "I want you to listen carefully. You need to save your sister."

"What!" I burst.

"Let me finish. Before my capture, I saw her welcomed by the Westerners. They worship her. All I could envision was how that could've been you. That could've been you feeling the love of these people, not a girl being beaten by my damn selfish nephew. Then I thought it can still be you. I don't know how, but when your sister came to me after a brutal beating, she defended me and wanted my help saving you. I saw your chance."

"How can you speak this way?" I spit. "She's only out to kill me. She wants to secure her throne, and make sure I stay out of her way. And how can you speak of this so confidently to me? Do you know how betrayed I felt when I discovered you hadn't told me of her? You've claimed for so long that you love me as your own, and I always thought you wanted the best for me. Why didn't you ever tell me of her? And why did you never tell me I could be a queen?"

"I'm an Easterner. That's where my loyalty lies, and it always has. I do as I'm told when duty to my kingdom calls. I do want the best for you. And I try to give that to you as best I can within my limits. What good would it have done you, to know you have a sister? Would it have made your life any better? Would it have changed anything? No." He shakes his head. "Do you know what your sister said to me?"

I don't respond.

"She said, *Surely if she means anything to you, you know that her being here would be much better for her. How long must you watch her suffer under your nephew's hand?*"

He reaches over and takes my hand. I freeze. This is the first time he's ever touched me. I look around, panicked.

"Forget the king's stupid rules. Look at me." My eyes shift back to him. "Your sister cares. I'd tried to kidnap her, and yet she cared about how I was being treated. And she cares about how you are treated. You might've done wrong, Vera, but she can help you get back the good life that was stolen from you. She's your second chance at something good. Don't believe the rumors of her wanting you dead. Some things are spread to make war."

The sorrow in his eyes breaks me. He would let me go so that I can be happy. His words scream betrayal against the Eastern King, but I see something has changed, and he doesn't care.

"It's too late," I mutter. "I've killed so many. And she's on her way to the king now."

Bellek's gaze turns stern. "Then take back what's yours."

I KEEP PROVENA A WAYS BACK, not wanting to be too close to Bruce. I know I can't take Bruce down, not with that stone around his neck.

Now that Livia is being taken to the king, I will soon uncover what whispers the Woman of the Scree has been feeding the Eastern King these many years. Soon I will know the true madness of their plans. A chill sweeps through me, and it isn't from the snow-covered landscape surrounding me.

28

LIVIA

I'VE HEARD about The Wall, how massive and indestructible it used to be when magic was woven through it. Even without magic it has stood for hundreds of years—until now.

I stare at the gaping hole, an impressive feat that was said could never happen. And my sister, Vera, is the one responsible for its destruction.

I tilt my head from side to side, trying to stretch out the soreness in my neck. My captor is relentless with his travel; we've ridden for two days non-stop, and my body is screaming in protest.

Vera has kept her distance the entire time. It is unnerving being so close, and not to be able to speak to her. I'm sure she's only following to make sure I am delivered safely to the king. I was hoping Bellek would have talked some sense into her, but with the passing of two days and her not so much as lifting a finger… she has left me on my own. Even so, my emotions are twisted, having a sister near me who massacred an entire room. It plays over and over in my mind. How do I deal with that?

I shake my head. None of it matters. What matters are the people left far behind me. My chest tightens yet again. The image of Amah lying in a pool of her own blood flashes across my mind. Without me there to heal her, she will not survive.

Anger follows but it's in vain. For the past two days I've tried to unleash the dark side of my gift. I even tried to heal my captor, just to see if my gift works at all, but nothing came of that either. I know something is wrong. He is immune somehow. But that shouldn't happen—should it?

The assassin takes off again. Dread settles over me as we enter the Eastern Kingdom. The cold air from the West falls away and is replaced by a sticky dry heat. The change is sudden, and shocking. Already sweat starts to form on my neck.

Cover from the pines helps shield us from the heat, but it's not long until we pass through that small comfort, and come face to face with mountainous terrain.

Mountains of rock circle my horizon. They are almost beautiful as they stretch high into the sky, their tops lying hidden amongst the sparse clouds. To the north, a brilliant stone arena rises up from the ground, looking like an extension of the mountains that surround it.

Tufts of grass holding desperately to life poke out from the hard ground below. The sight alone leaves me feeling parched, reminding me I've had nothing to drink for two days.

Black Ridge Castle towers above us, muting the sun and casting haunting shadows. Images of different kinds of torture fill my head, causing the beat of my heart to quicken. I pray to the Maker this place won't be the end of me. I also pray my uncle sends someone after me—and fast.

We pass through a steady flow of people carrying on in what seems to be planned urgency. They ignore us, except for two who come to fetch the horses. The giant assassin dismounts, lifts me to his shoulder and takes me with him.

My wrists burn something fierce from the harsh rope he's used to tie a knot around them.

He takes my arm and guides me through a cave-like structure, then up into the castle. We pass through long corridors with vases placed neatly along the walls and lit torches between each window. The soft rugs under our feet mute our steps. It's as if the decor tries to balance out the obsidian stone that sucks out the light from everything it can.

I look over my shoulder and see Vera following behind us. The assassin jerks me forward. Anger rushes up and I grit my teeth. I can't let this place defeat me. I must stay strong.

Two large double doors come into view, manned by red-masked assassins on either side. I focus on my anger and prepare to face the king.

When the doors open, I see the king sitting upon a black, ornate throne. His robes are like dark shadows that match his castle. I had envisioned him to be a harsh looking man, and I'm surprised by blond hair framing an angelic face.

The assassin releases me, and unties my wrists before joining the king on the dais. The king and I look at one another, neither of us looking away. He smiles. "Welcome to the Eastern Kingdom, Princess Livia," he smiles sweetly. "Your travels must have exhausted you?"

"Of course, I'm exhausted," I retort. "Don't demean me so."

His expression softens. "Please forgive me. It wasn't my intent." He snaps his fingers, and a serving girl steps forward.

"A room has been prepared for you," he says. "I'm sure you are hungry and are in need of a bath. You will find my servants instructed to do whatever you wish." The corner of his mouth curls up. "Except leave, of course. Once you are presentable, I will come visit you. I'm sure you and I have plenty to discuss."

I deeply doubt that.

The serving girl grabs my hand and takes me away.

Glancing back, Vera watches me with a frown upon her lips. She was probably expecting me to be treated much differently —as was I.

I yank my hand back from the girl.

"I don't mean to be rude but my wrists are fragile at the moment."

"Yes, princess. Please forgive me, princess," she says. "Come this way; we'll be in your chambers soon."

Her small voice is kind and I feel shame for speaking to her so harshly. It's not her fault that she serves a wicked man. So I quietly follow, and try not to cause her any trouble.

She leads me to a large chamber with a fire lit inside. The furniture is simple, unlike the elegance of such rooms back home. No intricate designs or popping colors, only solid reds and golds. A plate of steaming food and bread are placed nearby. My stomach rumbles.

"A bath has been drawn up for you, princess. Right through those doors." She points across the room to another chamber. "Do you need my assistance?"

I shake my head. "I'll be fine on my own. Thank you."

"As you wish, princess. New garments hang inside the standing chest in the corner. They are yours. We took measurements from your sister so they should fit you perfectly." She turns, and leaves.

I rush over to the food and shove a roll in my mouth. My stomach grumbles in response. I finish off two more rolls and a bowl of soup before I peel off my dust-layered dress that's covered in blood, and slip into the warm water.

I soak as long as possible, letting the heat caress away the pain. For a hostage, my prison isn't as harsh as I imagined it would be. But I know these temporary comforts mask the reality of my situation.

When I'm finished, I braid my hair and look through the many gowns. I hope for something simple but I am quickly disappointed. It seems fabric was scarce for the making of these dresses, and I desperately try to find the least revealing one. Once I do, I slip it on and stand in front of the mirror. The neckline plunges down to a point below my breasts, making me fully aware of what isn't covered. I'm tempted to put the dress I traveled in back on, but it's filthy and tattered.

A knock comes at my door, and it opens before I have a chance to answer it. King Kgar enters.

I swallow back my nerves as he strolls over to the table and pours two glasses of wine. He hands one to me as his eyes roam over my scarce attire. I tilt my chin up refusing to let my insecurities show.

"Come, let us sit and speak with one another." He motions to the chairs in front of the fire. I set the wine glass down, having no intention of drinking anything he's handed me, and follow him over to the chairs.

He leans back and places one leg over the other. "Now, Livia. I'm sure you already know why I have you here. You must know of the prophecy?"

"I don't, actually. I've never been told the prophecy in its entirety."

His eyes widen. "Really? Interesting. Very interesting."

"How so?" I ask.

"You are the future queen, the heir of the most powerful queen in all the four kingdoms. It's surprising how much in the dark they have kept you."

He has no idea.

King Kgar stands abruptly. "Come with me."

Silent Watchers flank us the moment we leave my room. I keep up with the king's long strides as he leads me down a dark corridor; moonbeams cast a dim light ahead of us. Our steps lead us up a stairwell and into a circular room where a roaring fire greets us. A boar's head is mounted above the mantel, with a slew of weapons surrounding it.

King Kgar walks across the room and pulls back a curtain along the wall. "And here it is. The prophecy." It's a large tapestry with the four Guardians woven into the edges. In the middle, large gold letters reveal a prophecy that has been hidden from me my whole life.

On the first day of winter snow, take heed. True blood will be born anew. Be wary of the shadow, for death will follow. Bonding will save him and awaken what dwells inside. Together, nothing can stop them.

I read it again and again. I try to work it out.

"Prophecy is a tricky beast," Kgar admits. "It seems easy enough, yes? I see you working it through your pretty little head." He takes my hand.

I try to take hold of him with my gift. I close my eyes but I'm faced with a black wall. Nothing is there. I reach for the other side of my gift and feel its prickle, but the black wall blocks me. I open my eyes to find the king's wicked smile.

"How?" I ask. "How do you block my gift?"

"You'll discover I'm full of surprises, my dear princess. One step ahead at all times." He drops my hand and chuckles to himself as he walks over to the fire. "The prophecy you read states that only bonding can save him, and together nothing can stop them." He takes something shiny off the mantel, unraveling a long slender chain; there's a slim collar at the end. "I believe it means that if I bond myself to you in marriage, then together we will rule them all. *You* being the firstborn and rightful heir to magic."

I place my hand over my mouth. He is mad! I turn quickly, hoping to escape but run straight into the giant assassin responsible for my capture.

"Ah, Bruce. Do you mind helping me for a moment?" Bruce grabs my arm and pulls me over to the king. His fingers dig into my arm and I bite back the pain. He holds me in place as the king snaps a collar around my neck. "A perfect gift for my perfect bride."

"I will never marry you!" I snap.

"Yes, you will. Or I will hold you down to sow my seed.

You will not deter me from plans that have been in place for sixteen years. If I were you, I would play along."

"And why would I do that?" I seethe in anger.

"Because if you don't cooperate you will watch me inflict your punishment upon your dear sister. Although once you bear me children, I will get rid of you just as Bruce, here, did your parents."

Kgar snaps his fingers and Bruce yanks the chain, making me follow after him. I knew it wouldn't take long for the king to show his true self. I'm not sure how to stop his mad plans, but there has to be a way to keep this from happening. The thought of producing any children by this monster causes my stomach to roll over.

When we get to my chamber, Bruce loops the chain around my bed post and places a lock on it. This man killed my parents? Anger sweeps through me as I watch him leave. No wonder Amah headed straight towards him. Tears swell up in my eyes.

Kgar is cunning. Being forced to marry him drives my hidden fear straight to surface. I crawl up onto the bed and slide under the covers. The chain keeps me from lying comfortably. There is no way for me to escape this place, and I fear no one can save me. Tears fall down my face. I'm powerless and alone. Not even my own sister can save me now. The tears continue falling until sleep takes me.

29

VERA

THE MOMENT KGAR DISMISSES ME, I go search for Zyrik. My need to have his small arms around my neck drives my urgency. It's been too long since I've seen my Little Rik, and even though I can't save my sister at this time, I can at least breathe easier knowing my participation in her capture has kept Zyrik alive.

It was unnerving to see the king treat my sister with kindness. He knew I would take note, and the sly grin he gave as she was taken away confirmed that. He barely listened as I gave my report about the war and provided news of his uncle. He brushed me away as if I meant nothing. It was a first, and I welcomed it.

Whenever I pass by the Scree's chamber on my way to Zyrik's room, I always walk swiftly past to avoid her dark gaze and cryptic words. As I pass this time, I hear her door open.

"Vera?"

I freeze in place, and turn slowly in response to the sound of a man's voice.

"Marcus?" I notice the stub at the end of his arm, and guilt consumes me.

He takes a step forward, filling the space between us. His unruly hair and soft full lips make me swallow. I'm surprised by how quick my desire sparks.

"You are back earlier than expected," he says. "Did you bring back your sister?"

Of course he knew. "I did."

"Seems pretty shitty for them to keep the knowledge of her from you this whole time."

"Yeah," I say mindlessly. "Why are you coming out of the Scree's room?"

He looks over his shoulder. "Oh, I was just delivering a message." He steps closer and wraps his arm around me. I push him away.

"Marcus, stop."

"But I've missed you, Vera," he whispers.

"I've missed you, too. Do you deliver messages often?"

"Not really. I barely have anything to do with her."

The Scree's door opens back up and out steps the Scree; she wears a gown that leaves nothing to the imagination, and her long hair falls down in front of her, barely covering her breasts. She leans against the door frame with a wicked smile.

"Vera, you're back!" she purrs. "Welcome home, my dear. I see you've reacquainted yourself with my prized servant. Be careful not to touch him. I'm tired of having to rectify your mistakes. Of course he doesn't mind it at all. Do you Marcus?" Her musical voice grates on my skin.

I stare wide-eyed at Marcus; he winces as his betrayal is revealed. "I'm so sorry, Vera."

I take a step back and feel my heart crack inside my chest. The memories of passion and what I'd once thought could be love trickle out into nothing. I'm a fool to have believed he was done with the Scree. Why would he want to stay with me when he has this?

"Vera," he whispers.

Anger bursts inside me. "Don't ever say my name again."

My gift rushes up and I drop him to his knees. Fear gleams in his eyes, and I know I can easily crush him. Instead I ball up my fist and punch him hard in the face. I hear his nose crack.

Marcus cries out in pain. "Holy shit, Vera!" He holds his nose as blood runs out. I turn and walk away.

I allow myself a small moment to feel the pain of his betrayal. When the moment's gone I slam a wall up, and lock my emotions away. So many times I've experienced the pain of being alone. But pain is part of my life. Am I capable of feeling any different? Can I become something different other than the hard-shelled girl I've always been?

I reach Zyrik's chambers. The moment he sees me, he runs and jumps and I catch him in my arms. My anger fades away as I find comfort in this little boy.

"You are a sight for sore eyes. I've missed you so, so much!"

Zyrik lays his head against my chest and I reach up and caress his hair. The worst thing in the world can be thrown at me all day, but as long as I have this boy in my arms, nothing can take me down. Not even Marcus.

Zyrik takes my hair and twirls it in his small hands. I kiss his head and brand this moment into memory. I can never lose this.

I remain with Zyrik until nightfall and tuck him into bed. When I crawl into my own, I think of Bellek and my friends. I hope they find themselves safe. With Bellek back in command I'm sure they're fine. Tomorrow I'll speak to the king and see if we can send word to them to come back home.

I roll over on my side and close my eyes. Tomorrow I will begin my planning for rescuing my sister.

MY EYES SNAP OPEN. Morning light fills my room. I hear the latch in my door release and I scramble out of bed just as

King Kgar barges in. I straighten my nightshirt and stand at attention.

He walks over and caresses my face, then tilts my chin up. For once, I meet his gaze.

"How much alike you two look. She even carries the stubbornness of your brow." He drops his hand and turns away. "I'm going to marry her."

"Excuse me?" I quickly shut my mouth and bite the inside of my cheek. He turns back with a sly grin upon his lips.

"Oh, Vera," he says, "how I miss our moments together. Please entertain me. Tell me your thoughts. Let this be a chance for you to speak your mind without any repercussion. I'm curious to know."

I don't believe him. All I hear is "trap".

His brow puckers at my hesitancy. "Speak!"

"Why?" I blurt. "Kings in the Eastern Kingdom never marry. So why now, and why her?"

His mouth curls up. "Good question, Vera. You never disappoint, do you? It's true. We kings in the East never marry. We rule for ourselves. But the magic is back. And the rules have changed. Unfortunately, you don't have the birthright to give me what I need. If you did, there would be no need for your sister. I plan to create an army." His eyes sharpen with intensity. "Through my children, born with magic. I don't care to marry her, but the prophecy states I must bond to her to rule all."

"When will this wedding take place, then?" I ask.

"Today."

I blanch. That gives me no time.

King Kgar strolls over and cups my breast. I take in a sharp breath. "Don't think for a moment," he conveys, "that I won't have need of you." He twists his hand until I cry out, then he releases me and walks out of my chambers. Hate burns inside me.

I slump down on my bed. Today? I noticed the stone necklace he wore. Even if I want to harm him, I can't. I have to get creative. And fast.

I STAND OUTSIDE the doors to the throne room, waiting to be called in. The morning has gone by too quickly. The king was smart to tell me his plan at the last minute. I adjust the uniform I've chosen for this special occasion. The only thing missing is a red mask to hide my distaste.

Livia stands off to the side. She looks beautiful. Her face is painted delicately, a gold dust shimmering all through her hair. She wears a red gown made of satin, cut low enough to outdo the Scree. A silver collar gleams on her neck with a fine chain attached and held by none other than Bruce.

Bellek's words echo inside my head. That could be me. I know he meant in the Western Kingdom, but I am visualizing it now: married to this very man who has stripped me of my dignity and forced me to be a killer. Then to have to lie in his bed and bear his children. For once in my life, I'm glad I am me.

The doors open and I enter. The audience is quiet. They sit in their extravagant clothes, witnessing history being made. I focus on the steps ahead of me as I walk up the aisle. A man in simple robes stands next to the king. I've seen him before, many years ago. He's our High Healer, and he's here to solemnize the marriage. I stand to the left of the dais.

The High Healer clears his throat. "People of the Court, please stand to welcome the future Queen of the Eastern Kingdom."

Everyone stands. I watch Livia as she walks down the aisle to her doom. A sheen of sweat covers her brow, threatening to ruin her fresh paint. I admire how she holds her head up in defiance, refusing to let King Kgar get the best of her.

Bruce hands Livia's chain over to the king, then moves to stand next to the Scree on the king's right.

"We are gathered here this day so that you may witness a joining of two kingdoms in matrimony. With this marriage King Kgar will further the magic that has finally returned to our kingdom. May his bloodline have infinite rule and all kingdoms flourish as one."

Infinite rule? I'm surprised Maker Adon doesn't strike the High Healer down on the spot for his blasphemous words.

As the High Healer continues on with words of nonsense, I focus on Livia. She avoids the king's leering looks and stares into nothing. Livia might think she can get away with this behavior now, but the king will break her. But if she could only get that stone from his neck, she could use her gift. Come to think of it, I don't know her gift's power. Livia shifts her weight, and a bead of sweat escapes down the side of her face. I am sure I will find out soon enough.

The High Healer continues on with his telling of our history with magic. I should be listening since I've never been able to learn this information, but my mind strays off to what needs to be done.

I spent the night staring into darkness, unable to sleep, knowing I had to save my sister. I knew it wouldn't be easy, and if I should fail....well, let's just say I hadn't wanted to think of the consequences.

That's why I had Zyrik go hide in his special place earlier this morning. I made him promise to stay there until I came for him. He didn't seem happy about the arrangement and I had to reassure him that everything would be okay.

"If anyone here sees this union as unfit, let them speak now or forever hold their peace."

Dead silence fills the throne room. They know their lives would be forfeit should a single word be uttered. But I don't care. It is time.

"I don't agree with this forced union. I find it a huge mistake for both kingdoms," I proclaim.

Gasps ripple through the crowd as King Kgar turns to face me. "What did you say?"

"I said, this union should not happen."

King Kgar steps towards me and backhands me across the face. I feel a searing pain on my lips as his rings slice over them.

"How dare you, you ungrateful bitch. Your words mean nothing. No matter what you claim." He brings his mouth close to my ear. "I was going to save this last bit for later, but I will let you in on a little surprise. I'm in great debt to the Enchanter for bringing your dear sister to me, and I've decided to send him my one and only son. I've no need of him now that I will have other heirs to my name."

The king smiles deviously at seeing my pained expression. He has planned this all along.

"If you take him from me, I will kill you," I spew out in anger.

He hits me again, but harder. The force knocks me to the ground, and blood fills my mouth. My gift comes to surface, but I push it back knowing it's useless while he wears that stupid stone.

He kicks me in the stomach before returning to Livia and the High Healer. I remain on the floor, wheezing in pain. I turn to the sound of the patter of bare feet against the stone floor. Zyrik is running as fast as he can, holding tightly to one of my knives. Fear stabs through my chest. Before I can move to stop him, the king yanks the knife from his son's hand and lifts him up, dangling him in the air.

"You disgust me." He spits into Zyrik's face and slams him to the ground. A loud crack is heard as his head hits the side of the dais. My eyes widen at the gut-wrenching sound. Ignoring my own pain, I franticly rush over to him.

"Zyrik! No, no, no!"

I place his head in my lap. Already his hair is soaked with

blood. I apply pressure to his gaping wound in hopes of stopping the bleeding.

I struggle to breath. My Little Rik! I'm not accustomed to seeing his eyes look so lifeless. I search desperately for a sign to show he is okay. Tears burn my cheeks and I can't control the rate at which they fall. This boy is my light; he can't be dead.

The edge of my vision turns into a violet rage and I feel every hair on my body rise. When I look to the king, a shadow of fear passes over him. The crackling of my gift covers my entire body—Kgar has just lost his one and only gambling chip he ever had over me.

How many times have I wished to unleash vengeance on this man, to show him what it is like to have zero power. I gently rest Zyrik's head on the floor and stand, caressing the charge from my gift.

In my peripheral view the crowd begins to disperse as assassins come forward and surround me.

I grab a knife from my belt and flick it at the king. The Scree steps forward and brushes it aside with an unseen force. The knife skids across the floor. I release another. She blocks it again. Five more blades are released one after another. All are stopped by the Scree. The Silent Watchers come in closer, their weapons drawn. Surely they know how useless they are. Or are they?

One by one I latch onto them. I may not be able to harm the king, but they can. I turn their swords against the king. Bruce steps forward, brandishing his weapon. I send the assassins forward, and like a puppeteer, I grasp their strings to guide the attack.

I send them after Bruce. To my dismay the king takes this opportunity to escape with Livia and the Scree. But it doesn't matter. I will find them.

Bruce begins cutting down the assassins, one after the other.

Someone shouts behind me. When I look over my shoulder, I see a red-masked assassin throwing me a gold coin. I catch it and see a dove engraved on its face. I can't believe it! It's Bellek's friend from the mountain! Seeing that I recognized it, he rushes past me to put his blade up against Bruce's, just as the last assassin facing Bruce drops dead to the floor. Another assassin, who had been standing with Bellek's friend, darts after the king.

I rush back to Zyrik, and kneel at his side. The thought of never seeing his dimpled smile again, pains me. If he had only listened when I told him to stay put. I try to recall the last time I heard his laugh, but instead despair fills me. I lean forward and kiss his forehead.

"I love you; you are my life."

Bellek's friend comes over and kneels next to me. He places two fingers against Zyrik's neck.

I look over and see Bruce lying on the ground. Is he dead?

The man puts his arms under Zyrik, and lifts him up.

"Don't!" I shout.

"Vera, let me carry him. He needs help."

"But who can save him? He's too far gone!"

The man tilts his head to the side.

"Do you not know what your sister can do?"

30

LIVIA

I TRY NOT to stumble as the king drags me through the corridor. Soreness creeps around my neck as the collar digs in deep.

I can't believe Vera stood up to the king. Hope flutters in my chest along with the lump in the back of my throat. Seeing the agony displayed on her face when the small child hit his head will stay with me for a long time. King Kgar said the child was his son, but that boy clearly means everything to Vera.

I recall my desire to go heal him, but the king tugged my chain when he felt me flinch forward. Why wouldn't he let me heal his son? All I needed was to touch him and his life would've been saved.

Kgar tugs on my chain again. "Keep up, you wench!"

My dress and hair cling to my skin as I do my best to keep up with their grueling pace. He is following the Scree, who I overheard saying she must find a safe place to establish her portal link to the Enchanter.

"I don't understand why we're running? Can't you stop her?" the king snaps.

"Of course I can stop her! Do you doubt me even now?"

"I saw your doubt the moment she unleashed her power. Don't tell me you didn't feel it too? I was afraid this stupid stone would not protect me!"

The Scree hisses through her teeth.

"I don't doubt the Enchanter's power, and neither should you. So hold your tongue." Her anger casts a haunting shadow across her face.

A shout comes from behind us. "Hey!"

A unmasked assassin comes running up the hall. The Scree pushes her hands out and sends a blast of wind hurling towards him. He throws himself to the side, barely dodging the blast. Getting back up, he runs his hand through his hair and I instantly recognize him—it's Reddik!

The Scree sends another blast of air, but Reddik dodges it. The blast explodes against the wall behind him, sending chunks of stone scattering everywhere.

"Reddik!" I shout.

When the Scree attempts to send another blast of air, I lunge out and push her down. The gust of wind goes off course and shatters the color-paned windows, bestrewing glass across the floor. The king jerks me back and kicks me to the ground.

"Stay there, you bitch!"

Ignoring the sharp pain, I watch in horror as the Scree sends her final blast of air, hitting Reddik squarely in the chest. The force slams him against the wall and he crumbles to the floor.

I release an agonizing scream. My gift comes swiftly, snapping to the surface. The Scree cocks her head to the side. "Oh, sweetie, did you know him?"

Her mocking tone ignites a fire inside me. I push myself up off the ground. Kgar goes to tug on my chain, but I whip my head around, "Don't you dare pull that chain."

Taking heed of my tone he relaxes his grip. I turn my attention back to the Scree. "I don't know who you think you are, but I'm done seeing you and the king harm innocent people."

The Scree cackles. "My dear, I am a Woman of the Scree, blessed by the Enchanter himself. He protects me from the ignorant mistakes you people make. You might think you are done with me, but there is nothing you can do to stop me. I know what your gift is, my dear Livia. And I don't believe it can stop me. The Enchanter informed me long ago of you and your sister. He created the both of you with the help of his dear old friend, Queen Bellflower. You belong to him."

What did she mean he created the both of us? The Scree's lip curls up. "Let me tell you a little secret. When your father called on the Enchanter to help his bride bear him a child, I was the one who administered her cure. So who do you think made that concoction?"

My heart thumps loudly in my ears as the Scree continues, "I helped your mother drink the cup of Queen Bellflowers' blood. Her blood allowed the gift to manifest inside Queen Kyra and implant the magical powers of old inside her offspring. Your healing gift cannot stand up against the Enchanter's power, so stop being a child, and do as you're told."

I smile sweetly as the Scree sneers down her nose. She has no idea that beneath my skin I have been caressing a different spark of my gift.

"Well, I have a secret as well, a gift your Enchanter doesn't even know about." I lurch forward and grab hold of her arm. Her eyes widen in surprise. "Death."

I release my gift and her body stiffens before crumbling to the floor. Then to my surprise, her skin changes color to gray. I step back as her skin continues to transform. It wrinkles and sags to her bones, then flakes away. Her once lustrous locks fade to white as my gift reveals her true age. Her body continues to waste away until she is but a pile of dust.

My mouth hangs open in shock.

The chain to my collar slackens as King Kgar darts hurriedly away. I rush after him and grab hold of his robes.

"Please don't kill me. I'll do anything. If you want to leave, you're free to go. Just please, don't kill me." He falls to his knees, begging for his life. His pathetic behavior doesn't surprise me. I grab hold of his necklace and snap it off his neck. In that moment, he whips up and pushes me to the ground before running off down the hall. But he doesn't get far before freezing in place.

"Where do you think you're going?"

Vera comes running up the corridor along with a masked assassin who is carrying the limp body of the small child. He stops near Reddik as Vera quickly runs to my side.

A pulling sensation draws me towards her and a strange feeling passes over me. Suddenly I know what to do. I grab Vera's hand. Her eyes flash to mine and the room around us disappears.

31

GOLDEN MIRROR

THE MOMENT THE SISTERS TOUCH, thunder claps across the entire four kingdoms. All over people feel the ground shake. Most continue on with their activities without giving it a second thought. Others, however, know the meaning and weep.

Livia and Vera stand, hands together; mist, in brilliant shades of violet and blue, shrouds them. They look around, taking in their dream world from a common side.

Vera: *What did you just do?*

Livia: *I believe we bonded.*

Vera: *Bonded?*

Livia: *Didn't you feel it? Like something snapping into place the moment I touched you?*

Vera: *I did feel something. Yes, I feel complete, like I've discovered the missing piece to a puzzle.*

Livia smiles.

Vera: *Where's the golden mirror?*

The mist parts, revealing the antique mirror. The sisters look to one another, and their brows rise.

Livia: *There has to be a connection in our minds that keeps bringing us to this place. What do you know about the magic of old?*

Vera: *Not much.*

Livia: *Well, I tried to find information about this mirror. Apparently, it's a relic from Guardian Pynth that's been handed down from ruler to ruler. The last to have acquired the mirror was Queen Bellflower.*

Vera: *Now her, I do know.*

Livia: *Well, when she and the magic disappeared, so did the mirror.*

Vera: *It seems strange that it showed up in a dream.*

Livia: *Well, no one knows where the mirror went. Wherever it was, it seems to have found us through the magic.*

Livia tells Vera what the Scree said, and about the prophecy.

Vera: *Our mother drank Bellflower's blood? Why would she do such a thing?*

Livia: *She was barren, and desperate to conceive.*

Vera: *But to drink blood?*

Livia: *I know; I am not even sure I would be willing to do that. Anyway, soon after, the Enchanter must have planted that prophecy in the king's ear, making it seem that magic would return through Queen Bellflower's heirs. I believe the Enchanter had a plan and knew what he was doing. When the Scree confessed how magic came to us, it all made sense. The Enchanter can't leave his temple, so why not use King Kgar to bring forth his plan—to breed for himself an army of the gifted.*

Vera: *But why would the Enchanter need an army? Why would he be willing to trust his fate to someone like King Kgar?*

Livia: *I don't know. Maybe he thought it would help him break his curse. Using King Kgar was the only way for him to have someone do his bidding. He knew the Western and Northern King-doms wouldn't help. King Kgar already wanted ultimate power, so why not use the king's goals? The Enchanter has nothing but time on his hands.*

Vera: *And he started by planting the Scree at the king's side to manipulate him. So he was able over time to guide the king to where* *he could collect us, and hand us over. The Enchanter is more cunning than the king after all. I should've known.*

Livia: *How could you? I'm sure the king didn't give you time to think about what the Enchanter might be plotting.*

Vera: *No, he didn't. My life has been spent trying to survive. It's still shocking that he never told me of you. That's why it was so hard for me to believe you.*

Livia grabs Vera's other hand.

Livia: *Vera, I never knew of you either. I was furious when I found out. Especially after I uncovered the true identity of my parents. I thought that was going to be the biggest shock of my life. When I discovered where you had been the whole time, my heart broke for you. Our people abandoned you. I wanted you to know, Vera, even though I had never met you, that I hoped we would find one another and become the best of friends. To know I had a sister with the same blood as my own made me feel like I wasn't alone anymore.*

Vera feels something break inside her. This whole time she's thought of her sister as this manipulative monster. But here she is, standing in front of her, and baring her soul for Vera to see. How could Livia have had an instant positive feeling about someone she'd never met? Vera feels a pureness from Livia that somehow feels familiar. She can't quite put her finger on it.

Something moves inside the mirror.

Livia: *Did you see that?*

Vera nods. Still holding hands, they both go over to look into the mirror. A bright light flashes out from the glass. A woman with long, dark hair and pale skin appears; she stares out with the same bright violet eyes as the twins.

Livia: *Queen Bellflower?*

The queen doesn't respond. It's as if she's looking beyond them, as if the girls are not there.

Vera: *Isn't she supposed to be dead?*

Suddenly, the queen speaks in a distant tone.

Queen Bellflower: *On the eve of Hellbore, they will come. Three shall perish, one must decide. Travel through the sands of time, or die. The one marked will set her free.*

Queen Bellflower fades away and the mirror's reflection stands empty.

Vera: *What does that mean?*

Livia: *It sounds like a warning.*

Vera: *Well, to be honest, I don't like the sound of it.*

Vera looks down at their entwined hands. She sees the scars that line her own and the smooth skin of her sister. The scars Vera wears were to protect a small boy—realization finally dawns on her. Zyrik! Livia's pureness is the same as Zyrik's!

Vera: *Livia we must get back to Zyrik! I was told your gift is healing—is it true?*

Livia studies her sister with sad eyes. She can't ignore the desperate hope pouring out of Vera. She sees the brutal scars on her sister's hands and arms; she knows the nightmarish things Vera has had to endure in her life. Livia closes her eyes and pushes her gift into Vera.

Vera's eyes widen as she feels the warm tingle of her sister's gift. She watches as her scars slowly fade away, until all the marred flesh on her body is healed.

When Livia finishes, she opens her eyes and sees tears running down Vera's face. Vera doesn't realize they are falling until Livia reaches up and wipes them away. Vera can't believe her sister has just healed her brutal scars. The wall that was built up inside her chest completely breaks away.

A flash of light reflects off the mirror and a whirling wind encircles the sisters. Their hair dances around them as the mist returns and trickles into their skin. The bond they felt earlier becomes unbreakable.

They can't deny the bond that has formed between them. They embrace one another for the first time in their lives. The king had it all wrong. The bonding that needed to happen for magic to thrive wasn't between man and woman, but between two sisters bearing the magic of old.

Vera: *For so long I lived with those scars, letting them define me. I can't believe they are gone. No longer do I have to be reminded of those painful memories.*

Livia: *Vera, I can't promise that I can save the boy, but I will try. I will do everything I can as long as there's a pulse inside him.*

Vera: *That's all I ask.*

Livia: *It's up to you to decide what to do with the king. I'll support whatever decision you make. I know you are healed physically, but I also know you have scars deep within that I cannot heal. Only time can heal those.*

Vera knows the king needs to pay for his tyranny and for the torture he doled out to her all these years. Her sister might have shown her love and helped break down the walls around her heart, but the anger that has been built up is still there, unconstrained.

Livia releases Vera's hands and reality comes whirling back.

32

VERA

KGAR REMAINS FROZEN IN PLACE, a terrified expression on his face. I allow my anger to flood back as Livia rushes to Zyrik's side. My gift sparks at my fingertips. This time there's a fullness to my gift that wasn't there before. It feels stronger.

My lips rise in a snarl. "Well, it seems you've found yourself alone and unguarded, and facing a very angry girl."

The king's expression shifts back into his well-practiced outrage. "You think you have power over me? I own you and your sister. Remember, you signed a contract. If you kill me, your life is forfeit to the Enchanter." He looks past me to Zyrik. "And the other part doesn't matter."

I flick my wrist, cutting off his air supply. I don't want to hear his voice any longer. He grabs at his throat and makes a strangled, choking sound. I smirk as he falls to his knees.

"No one owns me," I say. "Not you, not the Enchanter. No one."

He gurgles out what seems to be an irate response, but I hold his tongue.

"I don't care what you think you need to say. I'm done hearing you speak and I'm done living under your thumb. The memories I have are what others would call nightmares.

Your hands will no longer touch me, nor will they anyone else."

I welcome the sound of his hands crackling as I shatter them. Kgar's face scrunches up in pain. If I weren't holding his tongue, he would be screaming at the top of his lungs.

"You will no longer kick me or beat me down like an animal."

He crumples over, his legs fracturing into a thousand pieces. He writhes in pain, and moans like the creaking of a rusty door. Tangled up in his oversized robes, he attempts to crawl away on his elbows. If the councilmen could see him now, crying and crawling like a baby...

I have no love for this man, and torturing him feeds those desires I've had every day, that I've so longed to satisfy—to bring revenge down upon him.

For years this man has made me hate. It's time for me to end it all. I pluck a knife from my belt and walk over to the king, who is trying to squirm away.

"You deserve many years of pain and torture for what you've done to me and to Zyrik. So I hold this knife for Zyrik, to finish what he wants from you: an end to your evil, cunning ways."

King Kgar shakes his head, and his eyes are pleading as I plunge the knife deep into his chest. I watch the light slowly leave his eyes before I bring the knife back out. Kgar slumps onto his side. Just in case the knife hasn't hit the right spot, I snap his neck with a single thought. His body jerks, then stills. Without a question or a doubt, he's dead.

Broken glass crunches under my boots as I run over to Livia. I wipe the bloody knife off on my threads and return it back to my waist.

"How is he, Livia?"

"She can't hear you." The man's name is Kamon. He introduced himself as he was running with me to find Livia. He scoots over and pats the ground next to him. "Come, sit and wait while she works her magic."

I glance over at an injured man sitting on Kamon's other side. Unlike Kamon, he doesn't wear his mask.

"Who's that?"

"Oh, him? No one important. He's here for her." He points to Livia, and then motions me to come and sit. I shake my head, and he shrugs his shoulders. "His pulse was gone by the time she got here. I'm unsure what she's doing, but whatever it is, it's not working," he says.

I kneel down by Zyrik's side. Livia's hands are on his chest and beads of sweat are running down her brow and upper lip. My heart sinks knowing she has been at this for awhile, and nothing has happened.

I place my hand on top of hers, hoping I can lend her some of my strength. I reach out tentatively with my gift, but nothing happens. My head hangs down in defeat. I'd thought something might happen. But there was no wind or flash of light, just the sound of my heart thumping inside my chest. I leave my hand on top of hers. If anything, for comfort.

Kamon takes a deep breath, "If nothing happens soon, we'll have to get going. I'm sure there are more assassins who'll be heading this way."

I can tell he's trying to be gentle, but I don't want to listen, even if he is right.

Livia's hand warms and my eyes snap to hers. She's staring at me with the biggest smile on her face. I feel Zyrik's chest rise, and I glance back down.

"He's breathing!" I burst into tears as I reach across and grab Livia in a tight embrace. "You did it! Oh, thank the Maker, you did it!"

"I wasn't sure if it was going to happen," Livia confesses. "I was so close to giving up. That is until I felt something push my gift along. It was the strangest feeling. It coated my thoughts and I was able to grab his life strings and place them delicately back together.

"It was me," I cry. "I pushed my gift through you."

"Well, it worked. Together, we brought him back."

A thundering noise roars below us.

Kamon jumps to his feet. "We must go now!"

Livia looks over at the hunched man against the wall. "Reddik!"

Reddik? The Regent's right-hand man? He slowly lifts his head and gives Livia a weak smile. She places her hands on his head and closes her eyes. I look to Kamon who only shrugs his shoulders yet again, before gathering Zyrik in his arms.

Reddik's painful expression fades away and he pulls Livia to him, kissing her firmly on the mouth.

"Okay, you two love birds," Kamon interrupts, "we have to get out of here."

We sprint after Kamon who leads us down into the kitchens, then takes the stairs to the empty corridors below. How does he know about this part of the castle?

We enter a chamber. Reddik runs ahead and pushes a grate aside, near the fireplace. He helps Kamon guide Zyrik down the steps; Livia and I follow. When my boots hit wet stone, I realize we are in the underground drainage tunnels.

"Genius."

"I'll remember you said that," Kamon calls back.

I grin.

We continue through a labyrinth of twists and turns until Kamon leads us outside. We're near where the castle butts up to the mountain. He takes us to a small opening, with a fissure that cuts deep inside it.

"Is that where you came from?" I ask.

He nods. "There are two horses waiting on the other side. Reddik, get the princess back to her people. She's not safe here."

"They're Vera's people too," Livia presses. "And she isn't safe either."

Kamon looks to me and I give him a subtle shake of my head.

"Look, Livia," I begin. "I know you want me to come home. But I am not sure I am ready. Not yet. There is so much for me to figure out right now."

Tears well up in Livia's eyes. "But you're my family. There is so much we have already missed out on with one another."

I take her hands. "I promise I will come visit soon. We have the rest of our lives to get to know each other. And we have our dreams."

As Livia looks over to Reddik, I see light bounce off the collar around her neck. Grabbing my knife, I push her hair to the side. She freezes.

I huff out a laugh. "Don't worry, you can trust me." I slide the knife in the latch and pop it open. The collar and chain fall away to the ground.

"Thanks, Vera," she says.

"No, thank you, Livia. For all you've done for me. I owe you so much for the lives you saved today, including my own."

I'll always be grateful to her for tearing down my walls with her love. I've never felt more free.

When she and Reddik leave, I look to Kamon. Zyrik is still in his arms with his head resting on Kamon's shoulder.

"Where do we go from here?" I ask.

"To the end of the world, if that's what you want."

I roll my eyes and laugh. If he only knew that's exactly where I need to go. Someone has to stop the Enchanter before he comes looking for me. It might as well be me.

33

LIVIA

ONE MONTH Later

THE WILLOW STOOD HERE for countless years, a skeleton of what it once was. Now it blossoms again, full of violet buds, and whispers of wind moving its timeless boughs.

I stand in the top tower of the Willow Sisters Temple and look down to Willow Round. Thousands of people are gathered, some of whom have traveled from the farthest parts of our kingdom. Even dignitaries from the North have came to celebrate this day of my coronation.

A soft knock comes at my door. A sister pokes her head inside.

"We are ready, Princess Livia."

"Thank you, Sister."

As the door closes, I look down on the cheering crowd. So much has changed since Reddik and I returned. We traveled back at the same speed as when I had arrived—full speed. We found thousands of soldiers from both sides scattered and dead across the fields. The dead masses continued all the way up to the castle. I'd never seen such catastrophic loss. The

Silent Watchers had retreated back to the East by the time we got back.

We immediately reported to Regent Grif all that had happened. He was shocked to discover that I'd almost been forced to marry the Eastern King, yet relieved to know he was also dead. He understood Vera's reasoning for not returning but hoped she would come soon.

News of my return spread like fire, and Queen Bellflower's song had been sung all through the streets, drifting through the city on a soft breeze. It made me think of seeing the queen in the golden mirror, and of the cryptic message that she told. I plan to share it with Scholar Eli in hopes he can shed some light on its meaning.

Regent Grif said an earthquake awoke The Willow, and shortly thereafter it sprouted buds. The tree is once again alive. This, of course, prompted me to explain the bonding that happened between Vera and me. Regent Grif found that interesting, and wondered what else the magic had awakened.

My door opens back up. Amah steps inside and gently closes it behind her. I sigh—My Amah.

I rushed to her side when I found out she was alive, and was able to mend her back to health. Then she resigned as my caretaker, telling me I no longer needed her. We had a long talk about a lot of things. She decided she would take a much needed journey after I was crowned queen. We cried in each other's arms, knowing we would always love one another through this difficult time.

"You look beautiful, Livia."

Her eyes gleam as she takes in the high neck gown that flows down past my waist. A material with a soft grey sheen lies over a darker grey layer underneath, bringing out the brightness of my violet eyes.

"Thank you, Amah. I wish my parents were here to see me

now." I look down to my hands. "Of course, I wouldn't be getting crowned if they were here, huh?"

"En Oli, your parents would be so proud of the woman you have become. And they are here." She places her hand on my chest. "Inside you."

She extends her arm and I take it. We both leave the sanctity of the room to head down to the ceremony. Violet Guards line the walls all the way to the sanctuary. They stand at attention, their faces beaming in admiration. The last guard I see is Cam.

He tried to resign as my protector, but I wouldn't hear of it. I told him I was sure he would do better next time, and if not, I would send Reddik after him. I remember his booming laugh and the promise he gave shortly after.

Which brings me to Reddik. Every night since our return, we have met next to the tree in the Queen's Garden. Some nights we talk until we have nothing left in us, while other nights we don't say a single word. We have found a love and respect for one another that I know will last for a very long time. I can still feel the touch of his arms around me and his breath in my hair. I will always be grateful to him for coming after me and for all that followed. I told him of the golden mirror, no longer able to keep it to myself. He, too, didn't understand the magic but promised to help uncover whatever he could.

Amah and I stop in front of two large doors. I can hear the murmur of voices coming from the other side. Taking a deep breath, I find my calm. Amah faces me, adjusting my dress and pushing back some wisps of my hairs that are sticking out.

"You ready?" she asks.

Afraid of being sick, I can only respond by nodding. The nervousness of having all eyes on me prickles down my arms.

The doors open and Amah steps aside. Benches filled with hundreds of people occupy both sides of the now silent room.

The moment I take my first step a soft medley begins to play, signaling everyone to stand.

I continue forward and take another deep breath—why does the aisle look a mile long? I try to focus on all the smiling faces in the crowd. I spot Oliver and he's grinning wide. He waves excitedly, and I can't help but laugh. Standing next to him, grinning from ear to ear, is Annie. It takes everything I have not to run to her.

I look up to the balcony where beautiful voices sing flowing melodies, where Sisters in magnificent lavender robes fill the gallery. Their voices help me find my calm.

My uncle stands at the front. He couldn't look more proud. He told me this day would come and I'm thankful for how he's welcomed me to it.

I still wish Vera were here to share this moment with me. Last night we visited in the golden mirror. She wished me luck and told me not to get too big of a head. She laughed at my horrified expression only to tell me she was joking. It was strange to see her so relaxed, as I thought of all the times I'd found her angry. Freedom suits her well.

She is free from her bondage, and living in the mountains with Kamon. Zyrik is doing great, and has taken a liking to Kamon. He's not sad about his fathers death and seems thrilled to be in the mountains. He still isn't talking, but Vera is hoping with time he will come around.

When I asked about Bellek, she said they had been in touch and that he has taken control of the Eastern Kingdom. Apparently, when the king died, so did all the noblemen— something about a contract they'd all signed.

Vera also informed me of her own contract, and that she wasn't sure yet on a plan to handle the Enchanter. I told her I would help her with anything. I hope she doesn't try to do it alone.

Regent Grif takes my hand as I step up onto the dais. He guides me over to Prelate Rishima, who is smiling her welcome. I kneel before her as instructed, and a velvet pillow is brought over; it's holding my crown. It's a simple band of antique gold with a large purple gem set in its center. It's charming and absolutely perfect.

"Princess Livia comes forth this day to sacrifice herself willingly to the people of the Western Kingdom. She has already shown us her willingness to do all that's necessary to keep us safe and to share with us her precious gift. Livia, do you promise to always put your people first?"

"I do."

"Do you promise to help the people thrive and never neglect them."

"I do."

Prelate Rishima takes the crown from the pillow and places it on my head. I embrace its subtle weight. "You may stand."

When I stand and face the people, Hal and Kimber are in the front row. Kimber's jumping up and down in giddy delight. Lady Ella is next to her, and I'm surprised when her mouth curves up in a pleasing smile and she gives me a subtle bow of her head. I guess miracles can happen after all —and I will gladly take this one!

My eyes then land on Reddik. He smiles proudly and winks, which automatically makes my heart soar.

"I hereby crown and declare you, Queen Livia, ruler of the Western Kingdom!"

The crowd cheers loudly, "Long live Queen Livia!"

I welcome this new chapter in my life. I will forever cherish this moment. It wasn't that long ago that I was a simple girl, sitting high up in a black pine, hoping someday to see the world. Now I'm queen, and the world is laid out before me. My time is now.

QUEEN BELLFLOWER'S SONG

A fair maiden sat in her tower
  Her heart lay on the floor
  The child is gone,
  Her breathing no more

Oh' ring the bell, sweet Queen Bellflower
  Hark the maiden cries
  Ring ring my Queen Bellflower
  She calls high up to the skies

She made a choice, 'mid the snow
  Her magic is now gone
  Tears she weeps but of joy
  She is human in her bond

Oh' ring the bell, sweet Queen Bellflower
  The child breathes again
  Ring, ring my Queen Bellflower
  A mortal you now stand

Her final days are numbered

Oh' her child shall free
The magic that was taken
Inside a future queen

Oh' ring the bell, sweet Queen Bellflower
An heir will hear your call
Ring, ring my Queen Bellflower
Her touch shall save us all

Oh' ring the bell, sweet Queen Bellflower
Her life is yours forevermore
Ring, ring my Queen Bellflower
We'll love you evermore

ABOUT THE AUTHOR

Rachel Crist resides in Broken Arrow, Oklahoma. She is married to the love of her life and has an amazing stepdaughter. Rachel works in surgery as a surgical technologist during the day, and becomes a writer at night. This is her first novel.

facebook.com/Rachel.Crist11

twitter.com/ChullRae

instagram.com/raechull06

goodreads.com/Rachel.Crist11

ACKNOWLEDGMENTS

First I would like to thank God for blessing me with this opportunity. Without him I would be lost.

This started off as an idea and blossomed into an adventure. Never in a million years would I've thought something like this would happen.

Thank you Sabrina Flynn, for responding to a simple message and the hundreds that followed. Your help through this eye opening experience has put me forever in your debt. Not only are you one of my favorite author's, but now someone I can call friend. Thank you.

Thanks to my content editor, Shannon Thompson. The first to find my many loopholes and to give me encouraging advice. Also, to Tom Welch, who combed my book to perfection with his grammatical skills. You not only helped shape my sentences but also took the time to help me understand the changes. I am forever grateful for your services.

My amazing book cover was made by Chrissy with Damonza. With this amazing design I'll catch the "eye" of my future readers. Thank you so much!

To Ron Frisby for the intricate details and development of

my world. The map turned out amazing and it's super cool to see the land where my cherished characters dwell.

To my first round of beta readers, who enjoyed my story each time changes were made time and time again. My mom, Aunt Vickie, Jo Rothhammer, and Autumn Graybill.

Mom, you have been in Livia's and Vera's corner in this whole process. I always looked forward to your phone calls after I sent each chapter. You would either be mad or excited — mostly mad because you hated cliffhangers.

Dad, you are my hero. I hope you enjoy this story as much as mom. Just ignore the sex scenes. Same for Bambi and Brett, the siblings I wouldn't trade for anything.

Mentioning my own family can not go without mentioning my in-laws. They, too, have been encouraging and supportive of my journey.

Thanks to my husband, Michael, who didn't complain a single moment in the whole year I worked on this. You started off by telling me to write it, and look where it took me. You are my rock and the patience you've had will never go unnoticed. Also, to my stepdaughter, Hannah. Thanks for asking for a story those many years ago.

And finally, thank you to all the readers. I hope you find this story as captivating as I do.